P9-DVC-263

Musicians & Watchmakers

Dr. Caulfield
MH 333

Musicians & Watchmakers

by

Alicia Steimberg

translated from the Spanish by

Andrea G. Labinger

Latin American Literary Review Press
Series: Discoveries
1998

The Latin American Literary Review Press publishes Latin American creative writing under the series title Discoveries, and critical works under the series title Explorations.

Library of Congress Cataloging-in-Publication Data:

Steimberg, Alicia, 1933-
[Músicos y relojeros. English]
Musicians & watchmakers / by Alicia Steimberg ; translated from the Spanish by Andrea G. Labinger.
p. cm. -- (Series Discoveries)
ISBN 0-935480-96-X
I. Labinger, Andrea G. II. Title. III. Series: Discoveries.
PQ7798.29.T36M813 1998
863--dc21 98-21585
CIP

Cover art and design by Natacha Dinsmann
Cover photograph of author by Victor Sokolowicz

The paper used in this publication meets the minimum requirements of the American National Standard for Permanence of Paper for Printed Library Materials Z39.48-1984.∞

Latin American Literary Review Press
121 Edgewood Avenue
Pittsburgh, PA 15218

Acknowledgment

This project was supported in part by a grant from the National Endowment for the Arts in Washington, D.C.

A Note from the Author

Musicians and Watchmakers, in its current form, saw the light of day in Buenos Aires at the end of 1971 in the *Narradores de Hoy* collection, which was directed by Luis Gregorich at the Centro Editor de América Latina. It placed as a finalist in the Barral (Barcelona) and Monte Avila (Caracas) competitions. It's my first published book. But it was preceded by a number of separate writings that I will someday revise (motivated by that same pleasure one gets in looking over yellowed photographs taken by a box Kodak) in order to verify that the seed of whatever is contained in *Musicians and Watchmakers* already existed in those loose papers saved in sky-blue and yellow folders: the joy of leaping from reality into fantasy, from laughter to tears, from ridicule to outrage: a stroll through the fragile galleries of delirium.

But one thing that does not appear in any of my earlier, unpublished work is the theme of *Musicians and Watchmakers*. Even though I began to write with literary intentions around the age of twenty, it was some ten or fifteen years later that the stories which were told in my household began buzzing around in my head, especially the stories told by my maternal grandmother. They had little to do with what I read in books in those days, particularly those of Sartre, Simone de Beauvoir, Albert Camus, Miguel de Unamuno, Thomas Mann, Borges's stories, a bit of Bioy Casares, a smattering of Sabato and of Silvina Ocampo, a lot of Cortázar, the postwar Italians, Chekhov, Pablo Neruda, Boris Vian—a whole mixture of what we might call a "house salad." In those days I would fall passionately in love with whatever I was reading, with the kind of youthful passion that never returns. But when I would sit down to write, all the readings would disappear as if by sleight of hand, although I'm sure that they remained in those disturbing, deeper layers of my consciousness.

I suppose one day I woke up with the certainty that a distant and even unlikely French lesson that my maternal grandfather was taking in Russia (during which he noticed that the straw roof of that equally improbable "barn" in which the lesson was being conducted was on fire) was the only story I wanted to tell. I also wanted to describe the atmosphere in which I heard that story: the back room of the old "sausage" house in which we lived, my grandmother sitting at the table shelling peas, two divans known as "Turkish beds" covered with threadbare maroon quilts where my grandmother and an aunt slept, a 1911 issue of *Caras y Caretas* magazine, the Ollendorff method for teaching English through crazy dialogues in which a man asks another one if he's cold and the other one answers that he doesn't like fish. There, in that poor room with its high transom, facing the patio where my grandmother's enormous underpants hung from the clothesline along with the slightly bluish white sheets, a shade that was achieved by using "bluing," a blue tablet made of who-knows-what mysterious substance that lent the teachers' smocks their funereal hue—there is where I witnessed the snow melting in Kiev in springtime. I saw my eleven-year-old grandmother crossing the sea to come to Buenos Aires; I saw her taste a banana for the first time aboard the ship; and I felt the tremendous shock she felt when, also for the first time, she saw a Black sailor on deck.

All this was just a starting point. Writing the book was like turning on a faucet.

Something that probably doesn't appear in *Musicians and Watchmakers* is the lingering concern that shows up in my later works over how to say this, that, or the other thing. I used to have, and still do, unconditional love for my native language, the Argentine Spanish of the Río de la Plata area, middle-class, but with pretensions of intellectualism. Nevertheless, I have serious hesitations whenever I have to decide between writing "valise" or "suitcase." It's obvious that we Argentines worry more about whether they will understand us in Spain than the Spaniards do about whether they'll be understood in Latin America. This is always a thorny problem with no solution, one that I imagine occurs in all languages that are spoken in more than one country, or even in various regions of a single country.

But this isn't a problem that keeps me awake at night. Tap or faucet, something opened up in *Musicians and Watchmakers,* and the water has never stopped flowing, even though, like any writer, I too have gone through tormented periods when I thought the supply had dried up.

The humor in *Musicians and Watchmakers* also comes from my back patio, without underestimating the possible influence of other authors who wrote humorously. There really was no humor in my house, except for that which Aunt Amanda brought during her occasional visits. She had such a stimulating way of telling funny stories: for example, the one about a neighbor woman who couldn't speak Spanish well and went to the hardware store to buy a "nail to close up a hole" and ended up asking for a nail for her asshole. Amanda would grab her belly, she would laugh and cry at the same time, and I loved her, because she relieved the harsh atmosphere of our home and because she used to sing Libertad Lamarque tangos through her nose, which was, in her opinion, the best way to sing.

Music is omnipresent in *Musicians and Watchmakers*, although it doesn't have much to do with the title, because the musicians of the title, who were also watchmakers, didn't sing the tango *Scars*, or "You forget everything, my absentminded little bride." Nor did they ever sing the "International" in Spanish or any other Socialist Party songs, only ritual music in the temple. Music is in this book because it lit up my childhood and the rest of my life, and because in addition to telling stories, I would have liked to sing, to sing everything, from "There are three things in life: health, money and love," to "These Foolish

Things" to the "Coffee Cantata." In actual fact, I did sing: I sang in the protected intimacy of my house, and in the almost mystical atmosphere of the choir, together with other brave aficionados. We sang Bach, Monteverdi, Orlando di Lasso, Schumann…And writing and singing were one and the same.

MY GRANDMOTHER KNEW THE SECRET OF ETERNAL LIFE. It consisted of a group of such simple rules that it was incredible that no one other than she herself knew about and practiced them. Sometimes we would participate in the ritual, thus guaranteeing ourselves, if not complete immortality, at least a good dose of it.

One of the ceremonies of this cult consisted of boiling Swiss chard and eating it immediately, sprinkled with the liquid from the concoction mixed with the juice of two large lemons. In the most perfect enactment of this rite, you would boil the chard beneath a lemon tree. When it was ready, you would make a cut into two lemons that were hanging from the tree right above the pot, so that the juice that fell on the chard would retain its vitamins, without losing a single drop of its nutritional value.

My grandmother said that ninety percent of human ills came from constipation. At home we all suffered from it, and there was a continuous coming and going of prescriptions to ward it off. Despite her wisdom in this area, my grandmother suffered from constipation more than anyone else. Whenever she managed to move her bowels, she would walk around for a while with a big smile on her face, and she would tell everyone about it. She was even known to crack a joke, or recall springtime in Kiev.

Those springtimes came after really hellish winters. Just when it seemed as if the cold and the snow would last forever, one morning she would draw the curtains and watch torrents of water flowing past her window. As soon as the water had passed, the sun would suddenly burst forth, everything would erupt into flowers, and the woods would fill up with wild cherries. Sweet cherries, not like the ones we get here. And that's how it would be the next day, and the day after that. Not like here, with these springtimes that don't even know what they are.

That's how my grandmother would describe her native land, whenever the activity of her bowels put her in a good frame of mind.

I

I DON'T KNOW IF OTILIA EVER DELUDED HERSELF INTO thinking she was pretty. Perhaps one summer afternoon, while she was crossing Nueve de Julio Avenue in a streetcar with her fiance, a good-looking guy who resembled Clark Gable and was younger than she. You probably want to know how she caught him. It happened at a dance, where she and her next-in-line sister each nabbed a boyfriend.

The boys were friends. They hadn't been in Buenos Aires very long, and they earned a living as best they could. They also enjoyed the usual pastimes of bachelorhood. For thirty cents they could have a wonderful time on a sunny day: ten cents for the streetcar to the public beach, ten to get back, and ten for a salami sandwich. Stretched out in the sunshine, sporting their wool bathing trunks, their little mustaches and their innocence, they would talk about the future:

"Hey, man, you gonna get married?" asked Clark Gable.

"Um,...no," the other one answered. "I'm gonna travel."

Nevertheless, the weddings took place only a month apart, shortly after the conversation at the public beach. Otilia got married first. (How the pretty girl envies her ugly sister's good fortune!) I witnessed Grandma's preparations. She stationed herself out on the patio of the house in Donato

Alvarez, next to a bag full of little rolls. She cut them all in half and smeared them with something. On the folding tables they set up that night on that same patio, platters bloomed with little rolls, bottled orangeade and beer. I don't know if there was anything else, because I hardly even managed to get close, and when I did, I had to put up with my aunts' sloppy kisses and tell them what my name was, how old I was, and if I loved my little brother.

Nor was I able to observe the glorious moment when the brides took leave of their family homes and acquired the privilege of being supported by their husbands. The guests piled up around the bridal canopy, which was illuminated by an electric bulb. Clark Gable and his friend were tall guys; they had to tip their heads slightly to the side under the canopy, while the little lantern rested on top of their Vaselined hair. Despite this minor inconvenience, everything turned out fine. On tiptoe, stretching out my neck to no avail, I heard the rabbi intone the praises to God which began the ceremony.

I was just a little girl, but I already understood that you were supposed to get emotional, that the jasmine-scented breeze came from the garden next door (because at my grandparents' house there were only some red wildflowers that didn't smell at all), and that more than one guest disrespectfully turned around in the middle of the ceremony to cast watchful glances at the folding tables. At the first of these weddings I learned something: I didn't have to stay until the end of the ceremony to get from the wedding canopy to the food tables. That's what I did the first time, and I nearly got trampled.

Some years earlier another marriage had been celebrated in that house, a marriage from which I was born, and three years later, my little brother (yes, I loved my little brother). After Otilia and Amanda's weddings, Grandpa got sick and I stopped going to the house in Donato Alvarez. I had no further news of him until they took me to La Chacarita cemetery (because my grandfather, an atheist, a socialist, and a vegetarian, was cremated according to his explicit wishes and doesn't repose among our other relatives in the Jewish cemetery). They didn't tell me before taking me to the cemetery that Grandpa had died so as not to upset me. We stood for a while looking at a little box which couldn't possibly have contained Grandpa. Otilia and Amanda didn't go to the cemetery on account of their "condition." My cousins were born, also a month apart: first the son of Otilia and Clark Gable. They went off to live in General Pico, and we lost sight of them for a while.

Thus ended a long and difficult period for my family, but one that was lovely and full of fun for me. I would sniff the cookies that Grandma baked in the kitchen; I would watch Mele, Otilia, and Amanda rehearsing didactic plays for the Socialist Party Theater Group; and I would see a windmill emerge on the canvas Mele was painting. The canvas didn't interest me as much as the palette, covered with all kinds of colored stains and peaks.

Otilia and Clark Gable set themselves up in a room, in which they crammed a double bed and a couple of little night tables, a dining room table with chairs, a wardrobe, a cupboard, and a side table. In a vase that she called the "centerpiece," Otilia put a bouquet of artificial flowers that she had made herself. When the Chipmunk was born (we called him that because of his chubby cheeks), they also had to squeeze in a crib.

Motherhood didn't make Otilia more beautiful, but it did make her fatter. It was no longer possible to visualize her as she had been during her engagement: skinny in her blue linen sailor dress, white spool-heeled shoes, and a mane of hair with little spitcurls on her forehead. Clark Gable, on the other hand, was even thinner than before, but still good-looking, wildly happy, and a great prankster.

Once in a while Clark Gable's mother and sister would come from Entre Ríos to visit the couple. As married women, they enjoyed a certain amount of leisure and could travel for pleasure. They had screechy voices, and they practiced a form of birth control that consisted of repeatedly jumping off a table onto the floor after "having relations" with their husbands. They were famous for the number of miscarriages they provoked: in that family no one had had fewer than thirty or forty.

Otilia and Amanda, by hook or by crook, had become married ladies. Otilia chose names for her children from the social pages of *El Hogar*. The same names as the children of Señora Peralta Ramos or Señora Martínez de Hoz. She avoided those that were too obviously Catholic, such as any combination with María. Amanda, who had fewer pretensions and who was more sentimental and a great interpreter of tangos, gave her children more popular names. They were called Evaristo, Azucena, and Greta. This last name, which might be considered an exception, was a concession to her enthusiasm for foreign actresses.

With the business of the names, a long family tradition was broken. All Otilia and Amanda's female cousins were named Dora; all the male cousins, Leon. To differentiate, they were classified as Dora, Dorita, Ugly Dora, Big Dora, Little Dora, Uncle José's Dora. Then there were Leon, Little Leon, Big Leon, Leon the Watchmaker, and Leon the Lawyer. When they all got together, there was never any confusion: each one knew very well who he or she was and who all the others were.

With three of her four daughter already married, Grandma was happy. At other relatives' weddings, which didn't take place beneath the grape arbor, but rather in rented halls, she had her picture taken with her daughters, sons-in-law, and grandchildren, all dressed up and with new shoes. I learned to distrust the smiles that abounded at those social events. As soon as Grandma returned home from the party and put on her housecoat, her true colors emerged. Her face reflected an existence full of suffering, yoked to the side of a silent husband and daughters who fought like wild beasts, feeding on their insatiable bitterness. The four of them were, according to what I overheard from their arguments, bitches, vipers, egotists, imbeciles, tightwads, and evil incarnate. I watched them, trying to discover those qualities in their faces, but without discerning much except that they were fat and ugly.

After each fight they would break off relations forever. But they got back together after each wedding and wake, displaying tender smiles, too much rouge, and their kids, and they eventually patched things up. For a while calm would reign. We'd organize a picnic. Everything would turn out badly, plagued by ants, mosquitos, and packed buses. "When poor people try to have fun..." Mele would say. She was the one who got married late. Like her sisters, she was very fond of dramatic scenes. Grandma would try to lift our spirits by telling us funny stories that happened to other people: Some guy's business failed and he ended up on the street; someone else's trip got screwed up; another one had to leave school for financial reasons; yet another gave birth to a sixth daughter. She would laugh until she choked, never noticing if anyone else shared her mirth.

The same things weren't funny when they happened to her. Then she'd fall into a bitter depression, the grayish circles under her eyes would become more prominent, and she would take the event as further proof of her ill fortune.

In spite of her own unfortunate experience, she was a great advocate of marriage. She advised her girls to go to parties wearing beautiful, very low-cut dresses, with lots of jewels (real or costume, the main thing was that they should glitter), and to keep an eye out for the boys. Mustn't be a ninny. She'd say: "Young man, I'd like to introduce my daughter." The victim, taken by surprise, had no time to consider that not only did he not know the person to whom he was being introduced (which in itself is quite normal), he also didn't know the person making the introductions (not so normal).

This strategy never failed. The candidate would blush, offer his arm to the girl, and ask her to dance. Her mother would sit down next to the other mothers, who peered at her out of the corner of their eyes. It was pure envy, since their own daughters stood like wallflowers at the other end of the room, pretending to be thrilled chatting among themselves, while the others were already trying on their trousseaux or pushing baby carriages in the park.

ON CERTAIN AFTERNOONS WE HAD VISITORS AT THE house in Donato Alvarez. My aunt and uncle from Constitución would come, give me wet kisses, et cetera, and ask that stuff about loving my little brother. Once they brought their grandson along to play with me, but he was coughing a lot, so I wasn't allowed to get too close. I watched him from a distance, sitting on the bottom step of the stairway that led to the terrace. When everyone was distracted, I climbed the entire staircase. When I reached the top, I lost my footing and tumbled down to the bottom, landing on top of Otilia, who was waiting for me with arms outspread. I hit her in the nose with the heel of my shoe. After that, she glared at me with hatred in her eyes applying rags soaked in vinegar to her injury. She didn't say anything to me because I was just a child, but I'm sure that, from that moment on, I too became a bitch, a viper, an egotist, tightwad, imbecile, and evil incarnate, like all the other women.

My grandfather, the only man in the household, didn't generally participate in the conversations. Everyone remembers how he used to give orders to his daughters. Whenever he noticed them looking very happy, laughing a lot, or acting goofy, he'd give them a laxative. He was of the opinion that all strange behavior was the result of intestinal disorders. "Do you remember," Grandma would say whenever she was in a nostalgic mood, "how Papa drove you crazy with Josselin tea?" and she would shake with laughter.

When Grandma immigrated from Kiev to Buenos Aires she was eleven years old. They sent her to school, where she learned Spanish very well. She sang tangos like a sick bird:

Sca - a - ars (trill),
Indelible scars from a wou-ou-ound...(trill)

She never spoke of how she ended up marrying Grandpa. She gave birth to her daughters quite easily, one after another. They always arrived before the midwife, anxious to be born and start quarreling. There were some very bad times. Unemployment. Evictions.

At a charity ball, money was collected, as it was for other poor families, to help them get a new house. *El Hogar* published a short article about that ball. Taking advantage of the occasion, several of the girls made their debut into society. A few courtships began. In subsequent social notes appearing in the same magazine, there were pictures of their engagements, marriages, and announcements of their first babies' births. The young mothers selected names for their little celebrities, the same names that Olivia's children bear, even today.

Before they were married, Otilia and Amanda were salesgirls at La Piedad department store, where they extolled the beauty of the bathrobes and housecoats to their customers. Mele, the one who was slow to marry, never worked outside her home. Sometimes she would sew or do housework, and when she was done, she'd go off and paint. She painted flowers, sailboats at sunset, Dutch landscapes with tulips, and haystacks beside country houses. She copied them from some postcards she had.

On Sundays we'd all have lunch at Donato Alvarez. Otilia and Amanda's fiances would be there. The men livened up the atmosphere: they were talkative, they'd bring bottles of wine, and they'd sit you on their laps so you could demonstrate how you were learning to read. The women didn't fight. I would recite verses, taste Papa's port, and announce that I loved my little brother.

Engagements were announced as late as possible to prevent some other woman from setting her sights on the candidate. But there was also the question of tightening bonds with the future husband's family. Amanda was an expert at this. No sooner had Clark Gable's friend shown signs of weakening, and demonstrated that, travel or no travel, he was headed straight for the altar, Amanda began to visit her future sisters-in-law.

I accompanied her on the first visit, because the presence of a child makes these situations more comfortable. Most of the time is spent giving the kid candy, making her recite little poems, asking her idiotic questions and comparing her with other children in the family.

Clark Gable's friend had two old-maid sisters: Lia, who was very skinny and washed-out, and Marta, who was much younger with curly hair and a protuberant lower lip, and who blushed at anything at all. Lia had a very peculiar way of pronouncing her *l*'s and *r*'s. They sounded like a *w*, as in "wolf." She was the one who opened the door for us, made us cross a darkish patio, and enter a room whose door was flanked by a rusted alms box with a Star of David on its side, for contributions to Eretz Israel.

I had barely climbed up into my seat when Lia looked at me and said, "Oy, how dewicious!" and handed me a rather greasy pastry. But she was really more interested in Amanda. She devoured her with her eyes, from her wavy, brilliantined locks to her purplish-red nail polish to her aquamarine ring.

"Wook, Mawta," she called out, "Amanda and her wittew niece have awwived."

"Poor girls," Amanda remarked later. "They were so thrilled with our visit. "You should see how they live in that house…"

THE HUSBANDS WEREN'T AFFECTED BY THE DRAMATIC scenes between the sisters. Clark Gable, for example, always got up in a good mood to go to his little job. He was, Grandma said, a little worker. "A little worker with a little salary that doesn't amount to anything." And the corners of her lips would tremble with incipient laughter.

Let's get back to Clark Gable, who has just heard the alarm go off, the noise intermingling with the crying of his son.

While he proceeds to get out of bed, throws on all the clothing he can, and charges across the patio towards the only bathroom in the house, he sees his son hanging from his wife's tit. Otilia's face is concealed by dark locks of hair, revealing the vestiges of a permanent wave. As he collects his clothing to get dressed, Clark Gable removes a garment that doesn't belong to him: it's Otilia's corset.

When Clark Gable returns from the bathroom, the baby is back in his crib and water for mate is heating on the Primus stove. Meanwhile, Otilia puts on her corset. The only traces of her prenuptial slenderness can be found in her arms and legs. Her body, on the other hand, looks like a barrel. Otilia adjusts her corset, tugging on the laces at the sides until a ring of flabby flesh forms above the top.

Clark Gable looks away and whistles:

Don't sing, brother, don't sing,
For Moscow is covered with snow...

Clark Gable was a happy, generous soul. Whenever he was around, no storm could ever break. He would invite everyone to come over for mate and cookies, and when his luck improved, there would be all kinds of nice drinks and appetizers. He would laugh, recalling his childhood in Entre Ríos, his first days in Buenos Aires, the trips to the Municipal Pool, and his courtship with Otilia.

Every time Otilia would lose something (and this happened a hundred times a day in the chaos of their little room), he'd recite:

You forget everything,
My absentminded little bride,
Yesterday, you left over there, on the sofa...

We kids were fascinated by Clark Gable. We always asked him to sing or recite poetry. When he called us to the table for dinner, we followed him, eager to watch him scrub his hands to the tune of:

On that po-o-o-t
I didn't put the li-i—i-d,
I never di-i-i-d,
'Cause it gets den-ti-i-i-d...

ONCE AT MARDI GRAS THEY DRESSED ME UP AS PAVLOVA. I have no idea what it was that identified me as Pavlova. They took me around to show me off to the relatives, including my great-grandmother, the relic of the family and mother of my maternal grandfather. I was afraid to go see such an old person who might die at any moment. I prepared for that visit with the enthusiasm I would have summoned for an application of leech cups.

We walked down strange streets, I in my disguise and with a beauty mark painted beneath my eye, between Mama and one of my aunts. Papa walked behind, in his blue suit and stiff collar, whistling softly and looking at the treetops. When I saw him stop at a certain door and ring the bell, I tried to bolt, but they blocked my path and made us go into Great-Granny's room.

Because she was so unbearable, my great-grandmother spent her last days in a boarding house, far from her enormous family. Occasionally on a Sunday one of her grandsons would pick her up in his car to take her for an outing. Great-Granny sat in the back seat, leaving her grandson alone behind the wheel. Sitting as straight as an arrow, and without looking at him, she'd order: "March!" The grandson would start the motor, amused, just as her coachman used to pull the buggy out in Russia, where she ruled over her house, her land, her coaches, her horses, her children, the peasants who worked for her as nannies...and her husband of the moment.

Everything ended one day, suddenly. Those were the days of the Czar, the pogroms. The disaster was preceded by an omen that nearly cost the lives of half her children. These children were gathered in the barn, taking a French lesson...(When one heard these stories tirelessly repeated by the family, one never stopped to ask why. If French classes were held in the barn, it was because that was the custom in Russia, and so be it). My grandfather, who was already a poet, a philosopher, and a loafer by that time, instead of regarding mademoiselle, was looking at the ceiling. He was thinking about the cherries in the woods, about the tits of the wet-nurse who was feeding his little brother at that moment, and about his illustrious ancestors who went all the way back to "Kink David himzelf," according to his mother (I was convinced that in Russia they spoke my own language, but with an accent). Suddenly the young dreamer saw something on the roof. He opened his mouth and plunged into various additional reflections about things in general. Finally he knocked his chair over, dragged his sister toward the door, and began to shout: "Foigeh! Foigeh!" Everyone managed to get out just before the barn roof, in flames, collapsed on their heads.

Great-Granny didn't say a word during our visit. We all sat very stiffly in our chairs and on the bed. I amused myself by staring at a little jar of candies on the lamp table. When we stood up to leave, Great-Granny ran her rigid hand across my face (Good God! The enemas! The leech cups!), took the jar and placed it in my hands.

"Say thank you to Granny," said my aunt, pushing me forward.

"Thank you," I repeated, clutching the jar against my stomach.

As we were walking away down the path, I turned back once and saw her standing in the doorway, unsmiling and not looking at us. As soon as we turned the corner, a handful of confetti rained down on me and someone asked me, "Little girl, what are you supposed to be dressed up as?" "Pavlova the ballerina," I replied firmly. And the Mardi Gras went on.

GRANDPA SLEPT ON A SOFA IN THE CORNER. NO MATTER how early one arrived, everything was always in perfect order: the bed made, the floor swept. Grandpa read *La Vanguardia*, books by José Ingenieros and Juan B. Justo, and essays on vegetarianism. He'd sit me on his knees and make me spell out: *l-a-v-a-n-g-u-a-r-d-i-a*. Afterwards he'd send me out to the patio to play. He had a large mustache whose ends pointed up and whose shape he maintained by sleeping with something called a mustache guard.

Grandma slept in another room, which was very untidy. On top of the table, among dirty cups and bottles of medicine, you could see the twin arches of her false teeth in a glass of water, and her corset, much larger and more complicated than those of her daughters, with laces and whalebone everywhere.

Grandpa belonged to the Socialist Party. Firmly divorced from religion and family traditions, he devoted himself to instilling revolutionary ideas in his daughters. He taught them that everyone was equal, Jews and non-Jews alike. The little girls learned to sing the "International" before they knew "Rock-a-Bye Baby." He never managed to make them vegetarians. He had to content himself with eating his greens at the far corner of the table, casting an occasional disgusted glance at the stew that they devoured. He taught them to love work—not by example, however, since, thanks to a combination of bad luck, periods of crisis and unemployment, his ill health, and his brothers' selfishness, he didn't live a very active life, although it was full of all the appropriate maxims and readings. In their peaceful moments, the four girls would sing:

> *The sewing machine*
> *sings its hurried song,*
> *while the good woman*
> *sews and sings along.*

Mama was the only one of the four with any schooling. "We starved to death so you could study, bitch," her sisters frequently reminded her. "Studying is the only thing that keeps me from blowing my brains out for having to live with you, vipers," Mama would answer.

She was the first to get married, and, loyal to her father's ideas, she did so at City Hall. I was told this, since in those days children didn't witness their parents' marriages. On the wedding night, one of my classmates explained to me, the man puts his front thing into the woman's front thing and he leaves a little juice that makes a baby in the woman's belly. If he gets carried away and leaves too much juice, it could turn out to be a very big baby, like her uncle who weighed fifteen pounds when he was born and his mama almost died. It could also happen that, after nine months, when they sliced the mother's belly open and took out the baby, there might be a little unused juice left inside the mother. In that case, after a while, another baby would start to grow, and that's how you could get a little brother and always have to tell people that you loved him.

Grandpa's other daughters weren't as loyal to him as Mama was. As soon as they realized that they weren't going to get anything (I mean husbands) out of the committee meetings and the Socialist Party Theatre Group they went off to look for them, without any scruples whatsoever, at Jewish parties and weddings. I don't know how Grandpa, who was always saying that religion was the opiate of the masses, must have felt, standing before the lighted wedding canopy and listening to praises of the Jewish God at his daughters' weddings. As far as all his other ideas were concerned, Otilia very clearly and frequently said that he could stick them up his ass. Jewish husbands weren't "equal" to the others, they were better, since they didn't spend their lives playing pool at the cafe, and if they had a fight with you, at least they weren't going to call you a "dirty Jew."

"I'm so glad I married a Jew!" Otilia said. "You should see how Clark Gable worries about his wife and children! Big Dora's daughter married a Christian. She said she was "in lo-ove" [sarcastic tone]. And so? What did she get out of it? She's sure sorry now, poor thing! No, not poor thing, stupid thing! Because not a Sunday goes by that he doesn't lose every penny at the races. No wonder she has to suffer so much and sew for other people, poor thing, just so they can eat!"

As she spoke, Otilia finished polishing her nails dark red and waved her hands to dry them.

Evening was falling. Like flames, Olivia's nails passed before my eyes, and from the back of the patio came the smell of the sulfur that Grandma was burning to disinfect who-knows-what.

"DOCTORS DON'T KNOW ANYTHING," GRANDMA USED to say. "They're businessmen. They don't care about taking good care of you; they want to hurry up and finish so they can go on to the next patient."

She and the four beasts spent their lives consulting doctors, because no doctor was any good. They preferred "naturists" and homeopaths, because, as they would say, "they cure with natural things," although they never followed any of the treatments for very long.

There was one doctor whom they respected more than the others. He had his prescriptions filled in the only pharmacy in Buenos Aires where they had the Elixir of Eternal Life, and where they displayed the following publications in the window: "War to the Death Against Toxins;" "Wheat Germ, the Germ of Life;" "The Sedative Properties of Black Molasses;" "Live to Be One Hundred with Daily Visits to the Bathroom;" and "Keep Death Away with Ten Lemons a Day."

The doctor placed the utmost importance on anything that was consumed by mouth, but he combined his dietary recommendations with general advice on hygiene, publishing both in a brochure. Each patient received one of these brochures along with the appropriate medication for his or her ailment. It was recommended that one sleep with the windows open, even in the middle of winter; that one wash one's hands before eating; that one avoid all contact with other people's saliva (here there was a little note about the number of microbes that two people exchange with a single kiss); and that the following practice be observed:

"Moisten sexual organs with cold water every day."

After having been respected and consulted by the family for quite a while, this doctor was replaced by another one (Otilia's discovery) who cured all illnesses with different sorts of enemas, a method that she found truly harmless.

It was kind of a pity, because the first one was—how shall I put it?—more eclectic.

They would sit down next to our beds, look at us sadly and move their head a certain way, bending their necks first to one side and then to the other, so that their skulls bent alternately towards each shoulder. They would listen to the details of our illness and murmur: "Poor little boy. Ay, ay. Poor little girl. Oy, oy, oy." Papa's sisters weren't like my maternal aunts at all. They were long-suffering, respectful, and they didn't engage in arguing in front of other people. Sometimes they would run into the Beasts when visiting our house. "It's been so long, girls! Can you believe it?" They weren't as close to us as Mama's sisters were: we always looked upon them as the visiting team. As soon as they left, the local gang would rip into them without compunction, recalling the time when Papa's family was starving to death in the Jewish section of Entre Ríos. There were nine siblings. "Nine who lived," Grandma clarified, immediately bursting into one of her paroxysms of laughter. Grandma swore that Papa's mother fed her children a staple diet of angel hair pasta in milk until they were fifteen years old, and that's why they all turned out weak and sickly (my father's premature death confirmed that fact, according to her).

I don't know if the story about the milky soup was entirely true, but I can attest that my paternal grandmother believed that this was a nutritious childhood dish. All dried up, dressed in mourning, and with sparse white hair, she'd serve it to me in her kitchen, while in the dining room the adults entertained themselves with port and cookies. It was a sweet soup with milk skin floating on top and a few bits of angel hair pasta that got stuck in my throat. With considerable effort (because she could barely speak Spanish), my grandmother explained that the soup was good; if I didn't eat it, I was bad, and if I ate it all, I would grow up to be big and strong.

THE CHIPMUNK HAD ALREADY BEEN BORN WHEN OTILIA'S mother-in-law and sister-in-law from Entre Ríos dropped in to visit. A few days beforehand, Otilia received a letter. It said:

Basso, December 1, 1940.
My dear children Otilia and Clark Gable:

I'm writing to you from here to tell you that on the tenth we are leaving for there. Clarita and I are going, since your Papa and Clarita's husband can't get away from work. Don't worry about anything, Otilia—I'm going to stir up your pot and cook up a real storm for you.

Tell my son to get ready to eat like he did before, at least for a few days, because I'm going to make him the things he likes best. I don't understand how he can eat any old thing these days. As we imagine you won't have anywhere for us to sleep (I don't know why you don't come to live in Entre Ríos—Clark Gable could get a good job and you all could have a real house like regular people, so that if his mother came she'd have a place to sleep), we're going to stay with Sarita. But all day long we'll be with you, since it's been so long since we've seen each other.

I'm bringing you a few jars of honey for the baby, since they tell me he's cutting his little teeth. He must be very cranky. With children there are always problems and worries and headaches. I told Clark Gable, what was the hurry? But now that the little one is here, be careful to keep away the Evil Eye. From the picture I see he's very beautiful: he looks like his father.

Well, children, your mother sends a big hug and lots of wishes for your happiness.

(signed)

PS: Otilia, I'm telling you again not to worry—I'll cook up a storm for you.

Otilia's mother-in-law and sister-in-law stayed long enough to make Otilia start talking about the insane asylum. Like her mother and sisters, Otilia was afraid of the asylum. She believed that sooner or later she'd end up there, not because she suffered from a mental illness, but rather because of all the suffering inflicted on her by the egotism, viciousness, idiocy, and greed of her relatives. "You want me to end up crazy, but I won't give you the satisfaction," she told Mele when Mele refused to take care of the Chipmunk so that Otilia and Clark Gable could take their visitors from Entre Ríos to the movies.

Mele said she was tired of making sacrifices, that she had to finish up a painting of a weeping willow that evening, and at the river's edge she was painting a fisherman's basket full of dead fish, with their heads sticking up over the sides. It was going to be a wedding gift. "You've already established your life," Mele told Otilia in a bitter voice. "I haven't, yet." "And how do you expect to find a husband with that ragmop face of yours," Otilia hissed at her as she walked away.

Clark Gable wasn't disturbed by the contretemps. He brought out a bottle of vermouth and a few little snacks, and he laughed and told jokes until midnight, never noticing Otilia's sour expression. When he was a bit tipsy, he put his arm around Otilia's waist and began to sing:

My sweetheart was skin and bones,
skin and bones...

At twelve sharp the Chipmunk woke up. Otilia changed his diapers, amid shouts of admiration by her mother-in-law and sister-in-law, who couldn't contain themselves and kept pinching the baby's legs. With so much shouting and pinching, the Chipmunk began to cry even louder, so that when Otilia placed him to her breast, he couldn't grasp the nipple. With the visitors shouting advice, they turned him upside down, rightside up, on his side, they made him swallow chamomile tea, bundled him up, unwrapped him, bounced him in their arms, and finally laid him in the crib to let him cry it out. Three-quarters of an hour later, when he finally fell asleep, Clark Gable's mother had recounted how her children never cried, because she knew how to raise them, and besides, they lived in a big house, and not in a twelve-by-twelve room like the Chipmunk.

The next day they returned to Entre Ríos. Otilia didn't go to the insane asylum, but almost. She spent all morning in bed with a wet cloth on her forehead, and when Clark Gable came home for lunch, he had to change the Chipmunk's diapers and brew his own *yerba mate*. Just as well his mother wasn't there to witness all that.

If you feel like peeing at one in the morning and you live in a rented room that faces a patio with a bathroom at the far end of it, you have to bundle yourself up and brave the elements.

If this happens to you often, including when it's raining, and if you generally find the bathroom already occupied, you'll end up devising a less elegant solution. In my house we simply called it the chamberpot.

The chamberpot goes beneath (at the foot of) the bed, and is only to be used for urinating. In the morning it must be carried to the bathroom to be emptied and rinsed. Each adult carries his or her own (married couples can share one between them), and it isn't advisable to ask the maid to carry it because sometimes they put on airs and might dump you for something like that.

If there are various tenants in the house, you need to take a peek from the door of your room and hurry up with the thing while the patio is deserted. But it might happen that: 1) while you're crossing the patio someone could come out of his room and cross your path, or 2) in your rush you might tip the basin or trip and drop it, and you'd make a terrible spectacle of yourself.

In the house where Otilia and Clark Gable rented their room during the early days of their marriage, there also lived Vicente, a shoe repairman. He was an orderly man. Every day he would clean his room, brew a few *mates*, walk a block to the bowling alley where he'd practice his cobbler's craft until one. Then he'd close the shop, have lunch—always alone—at the luncheonette, return to the bowling alley where he would work until seven, close up again, and return home. He would hole up in his room with a loaf of bread and some cold cuts, and he wouldn't be seen again until the next morning. You couldn't have asked for a better neighbor. He was less bothersome than a corpse.

In the morning he would set out for the communal bathroom and if he saw the door closed he'd return to his room, only to try again later. In winter he went to the bathroom in his overcoat and scarf, with his towel folded over his arm, his toothbrush in his right hand, and a large gray pail hanging from his left arm.

Otilia had no question about the function of the pail. Her eyes gleamed like Sherlock Holmes's as she told Grandma about it. Mele listened, smiling, as she placed the finishing touches on an oil painting of a little Dutch girl standing next to a cow, with a different colored tulip on either side.

"YOU'RE GOING TO KILL ME," GRANDMA SAID. "YOU'RE going to finish off the few years of life I have left." She said this in a suffocated voice, weak and intense and tremulous at the same time, as she placed her fist on the table in a feigned blow since, according to her, she was so broken down, so worn out, that she didn't even have the strength left to make a proper fist. During these scenes she looked very hunched over, her hair in disarray, with a vacant expression and purplish circles under her eyes. After pronouncing each phrase she seemed to collapse, with her lower lip hanging out and trembling like a leaf.

Her phrases began in a low tone, almost a whisper, and rose up to a high pitch at the beginning of the last syllable, whose vowels were stretched out long enough to achieve (without losing the rhythm) an even sharper pitch than at the beginning. That is to say, an ascending tone:

> *You're going to k-i-i-i-l-l...*
> (and in a descending tone):
> *me-e-e-e.*
> (and again, voice rising):
> *You're going to finish off the few years of life...*
> (descending pitch):
> *I have...le-e-e-e-f-t.*

The fights Grandma had with her daughters were different from the ones they had among themselves. The beasts fought like equals, and none of them seemed lessened by the experience. They spoke plainly: "You want to screw up my life, you bitch, you viper, but I won't give you that pleasure." They were young, vigorous women who had nursed from none other than my grandmother herself and who had been nourished by a naturistic-vitaministic-anti-constipationistic regimen. Their mother, on the other hand, was old and quite worn down by the life she had led (always sacrificing herself to raise her daughters).

I never figured out how the fights began because I wasn't there (children should be spared violent scenes). I drew closer when the shouts penetrated the closed door and crossed the patio. Then I'd spy from behind the door, or I would go right into the room and no one took notice of me. At those moments the accusations usually referred to very ancient matters, and Grandma would be receiving the fatal blows.

The blows were almost always of the verbal variety. Only once did I see Grandma receive a punch in the arm. I waited to see if she'd be felled by lightning, but strangely enough, Grandma seemed to calm down with the impact. She rose from her chair (she almost always fought from a sitting position, due to her extreme weakness), and she left the room, rubbing her arm.

From the first fight I ever witnessed, during which Grandma announced, as usual, that she was dying, to her actual death, twenty-five years ensued. Only in the last few years did she modify her technique a bit. She no longer threatened to die, but rather she would ask for a cup of tea, grab the cup with tremulous hands, and spill the entire contents down the front of her blouse. A daughter would have to help her change her clothes, to keep her from catching a chill. Or else she would say, "All right, Otilia, all right, don't be that way." A clear wish for reconciliation. Proof that Grandma was tired of violence and honestly desired peace. Unfortunately, the one with whom she was fighting at the time wasn't Otilia, but rather Amanda. The confusion of names infuriated her daughter even more. "You pretend to be stupid," she shouted at her. "You want me to think you don't know who I am, that you've got me confused with that other snake!"

And it went on like that until that poor mother ended her sad days. According to her, she deserved a happier ending.

When my grandmother was young, everything tasted better. Colors were more vibrant, flowers more fragrant, and life was happier and more peaceful. Everyone loved one another and helped one another, and when Mardi Gras rolled around, everybody would dress up. Grandma and her friends would compete to see whose costume was prettier: this one was dressed like a cobra, that one like a rattlesnake, the other one like a fox, yet another like an army ant.

How those happy times ended, and how she ended up married to that vegetarian rebel, thus beginning a period of steady decline, what with her daughters' arrival and her husband's becoming increasingly theoretical, is something that no one cares to recall. Family pictures don't give us any clue. The four girls appear in all the photos, with ribbons in their hair and garlands of flowers all around. There are some snapshots of Otilia and Amanda at the height of their husband-seeking period, of the times they went to visit the relatives in Entre Ríos to see how the pickings were over there. And there's another one of the two of them, skinny and smiling in their sailor dresses, walking around Paraná, like the photos of Punta del Este in *El Hogar* magazine.

While Otilia and Amanda were in Paraná, the cousins who lived there came to Buenos Aires. But those country girls were such hicks, Amanda said. They thought that being beautiful consisted of being "white, flushed, and fat." The local boys would take up with one half-breed after another, and sometimes they even married them—when there were such pretty girls in the Jewish community! The more romantic of these rejects sometimes made a drastic decision: they slung their fishing rods over their shoulders and went off to Israel. It seems that fishing was better there, because the emigrée's mother, when asked, would generally reply: "She's fine. She GOT MARRIED," and show photos of the kibbutz and the new-born grandson. The poor mother would cry as she displayed the photos. With any luck at all, she'd become sick enough to oblige the daughter to return home with her family.

But it was a tricky business. Otilia and Amanda never even considered it, although they did have great admiration for those who emigrated to Israel. "They're idealists," they said. "Besides, they had no luck here, those girls."

"A DIRTY, IGNORANT LITTLE HALF-BREED WHO WIPES HER ass and then serves you dinner with the same hand." That's what Grandma had to say about servants. That was the reason she never had any at home, and besides, she wouldn't have had anything to pay them with.

Nonetheless, when the house in Donato Alvarez went to hell as a result of Otilia's and Amanda's weddings and Grandpa's death, Grandma and Mele came to live with us, and Grandma had to get along with the hired help. She wouldn't let them touch anything in the kitchen, and if by some accident, they did, she'd wash everything with boiling water before using it.

She said that the cleaning girls were as strong as horses, so no amount of work was too much for them. She couldn't understand why none of them ever stayed with us too long.

Whenever she suspected them of stealing, she sent them out to buy something, and while they were gone she went through their rooms. I remember what one of those girls kept in a valise that Grandma opened up while she was off on her appointed errand: a little package of sugar, another one of *yerba mate*, another of cornstarch and one containing a couple of carrots. The girl carried this valise with her when she went home for the weekend. Grandma took it upon herself to fire her and reported her action to the rest of the family. After railing against "those shitty little half-breeds," Grandma was reminded by Otilia that the one she had just fired had two little kids who were being raised by their grandmother. "So you see," Otilia commented, "she stole for the children." Grandma burst out in one of her attacks of laughter. That Otilia was so sentimental.

True, the servants were well fed, for fear that they might otherwise catch tuberculosis, "a danger" to us. Any one of them who coughed was fired on the slightest pretext as a precaution.

They slept in a little room at the end of the patio, far removed from the rest of the house. They had to cross the patio to use "their" bathroom, a three-by-three space that had a marble slab with a hole in it and a cold-water shower that didn't work. Every so often Grandma would go inside, holding her breath, brandishing a bottle of disinfectant that she would sprinkle so liberally that you could smell it from out in the street.

At siesta time, when vigilance was somewhat more relaxed, I used to escape to the servant's room We would sit on her bed and chat. She'd show me her things: beaded necklaces, religious medallions and images, a picture of her with a soldier taken in Rosedal, overpowering perfumes, rouge, mascara, a box of face powder. On the wall, on either side of the mirror, was a photo of Gardel and a picture of the Virgin with a sprig of wheat plastered across it.

When it rained, these interludes were even more delightful. The little room seemed more distant from the rest of the house. We ate pastries that the girl bought herself (they didn't get such luxuries in our house), and we talked about boyfriends and relatives who lived far away in the country. There was even one who didn't know—she didn't know!—how many little brothers and sisters she had. Which meant she was more or less excused from saying that she loved them.

In the room occupied by Grandma and Mele there was a door (now boarded up) that led to the basement. It was next to that door that I read *Voyage to the Center of the Earth*, lying on Grandma's bed. The voyagers descended to the bowels of the earth through the crater of an extinct volcano. I wasn't all that impressed by the voyage, nor the danger, nor the unknown depths plumbed by the protagonists. What did impress me was the fact that at the center of the earth there was an inhabitant—or perhaps several—who were invisible to the explorers except for their shadows. Then my grandmother walked in with my milk.

While I drank it I had to listen to her talk about how good milk was for me, how two glasses of milk a day would make me immortal, indestructible. On other occasions, boiled vegetables were the thing that would turn me into a horse. "Let's see now, you're a smart girl," Grandma would start in as she dug up a forkful of steaming spinach to "help" me. "Since you're so big and you know everything, tell me, why is it that a horse can pull a heavy wagon loaded with tree trunks?" "Because it's a very strong animal," I answered, as the mysterious denizen of the basement's depths called out to me. "Then," Grandma continued, "what will you be if you eat a lot of vegetables like a horse?" "I'm going to be a horse," I answered absentmindedly. Socrates got angry. "You pretend you don't understand," she said, "but just look at how your other grandma's children turned out because they didn't eat right, like children should: they're all sickly and weak."

Among my paternal grandmother's children was, of course, my father. His premature death strengthened Grandma's convictions about the deficiencies in his childhood diet. She didn't quite say "I told you so!" right at that moment. Out of consideration. But after a while she'd go back and harp on the same theme. I had to eat double portions of greens and other immortality-granting foods because only one half of me, my mother's side, was healthy, strong and immortal. The other side, the paternal branch, was weak, subject to all kinds of illnesses and death. And if I didn't believe her, I should just compare the Beasts, who were ready to devour each other or anyone else who crossed their paths, to my fragile paternal relatives: an asthmatic uncle who lived in a protective bubble, an aunt with liver disease and a sour lemon face (no offense to the lemon), another aunt with high blood pressure who could die on us any day, just like my poor father.

I thought and compared, again and again, and to this very day I don't know to which side I'd rather belong.

We called our paternal grandparents by their given names to differentiate them from the others. Grandma Ana never smiled, unlike the other one who smiled all the time. Whenever they were together at some family reunion, they looked like the two masks, Comedy and Tragedy, of the Theater of Humanity.

Grandpa José rarely smiled, if ever. My uncles would ask me questions and laugh at my answers, and when they had exhausted my supply of cleverness, they'd send me outside to the garden to play. I'd leave through the window, lowering myself into a wildflower patch that was full of red insects. One day, instead of sliding out carefully, I positioned myself on the ledge and jumped. Grandpa José, who was in the garden looking at something, began to shout: "*Schpeinel kohlum! Schpeinel kohlum!*" My uncles came running out to see what was going on, and they explained that my grandfather was very angry because I could have fractured my spinal column. They made me promise I would never jump from heights again.

I would have kept that promise if I hadn't noticed the ashes in that same garden the following Sunday. There had been a barbecue, with a great deal of eating, wine drinking, and general tumult. Afterwards, everyone went inside to rest. I stood there regarding the pile of gray ash where the barbecue had taken place. Suddenly I looked up and saw that one of my uncles was standing there. He had a terrible asthmatic cough that got worse every spring, at which time he would shut himself up in a kind of glass chamber that kept out the pollen.

"So?" he asked me. "Are you going to jump again?"

I looked at the pit filled with ashes. "It isn't so high," I said.

My uncle looked at me with a serious expression, and whistling noises came out of his chest.

"Bet you won't jump," he said.

One minute later I found myself in the hallway, surrounded by a bunch of people shouting at me and wanting to know why I had jumped into the hot ashes. My asthmatic uncle asked the same question.

I spent the rest of the afternoon soaking my feet in a basin of boric acid solution, reading the comics.

At dusk the house became lively again. We sat on the porch and my aunts served seltzer with musk rose syrup. The musk roses grew like vines on the walls of the house. We used to use them to make costumes for Mardi Gras.

"What costume can I wear?"

"You can bc a musk rose."

"And what does a musk rose costume look like?"

"With your butt in the air and no mask."

WHATEVER I KNOW ABOUT MY FATHER'S FAMILY AND their lives in the Jewish colony of Entre Ríos, I learned from my maternal grandmother, who, without meaning to, probably altered the facts a little.

According to her, the family lived way out in the country. A ship brought my grandparents over from Russia around 1890, or perhaps earlier. The refugees traveled all crowded together like animals, and there was hardly any water to drink. They had to suck it through a kind of straw that was connected to a barrel. I have no idea how they were transported from the ship to the middle of the countryside!

Once arrived, my grandparents looked at each other, and seeing that they weren't grandparents or even parents yet, they rushed to get married and get it over with. Or maybe they were already married in Russia; that point isn't really very clear. And right away my uncles and aunts were born.

Unfortunately, Grandpa José wasn't a country sort of fellow. He was a teacher, dedicated to meditating and teaching children the history and religion of the Hebrew people. Grandma Ana, on the other hand, became a Jewish gaucha. She did all the work, constantly giving birth to children whom she nourished with angel hair pasta and milk until they reached the age of fifteen. As soon as they grew up, they moved away, and some of them, like my father, never came back. He only came back to visit his family after they had moved to Buenos Aires.

Looking out a window of his house in Saavedra, Papa noticed that his sister came back from English class every Tuesday and Friday in the company of a certain girl

(Mama). This episode is followed by a fuzzy period containing Mama and Papa's wedding, my intrauterine life, and my birth in the maternity wing of Rivadavia Hospital.

I am, therefore, the result of a great deal of toil and trouble: relocations, uprootings, weddings that took place who-knows-where, in Argentina or in Russia, fights that began who-knows-why, crazy dietary regimens, readings from the Torah, and "religion is the opiate of the masses."

In spite of it all, one summer afternoon, before I had even learned to walk, I managed to have my picture taken, sitting on the Costanera in the shade of Mama's straw bonnet, feeding the pigeons.

Everything is milky-colored: Mama's arms, her bonnet, my dress, the pigeons. No doubt when the sun went down, we left the river behind and took a streetcar home, weaving through all the lights of Buenos Aires.

II

Even on the train they asked me if I loved him, and I answered yes, just as I had been taught. They carried him in their arms, and sometimes he'd cry, but what did I care as long as I was sitting next to the window, looking out at the countryside and the cows.

When we got to the hotel they changed his diaper and sat him in his baby carriage. Then he disappeared. They left me on the sand with my digging toys, and then they, too, disappeared. The other kids who were playing there were bigger than I was and they grabbed my sand molds. "They're mine," I said. But they said, "We need them," and they didn't give them back to me even though I repeated, "They're mine." Time went by very slowly as I waited for the grown-ups to come back for me.

The other kids laughed at the way I sat on the sand, because they could see my panties. They said I was posing for a photo. "Miss Kodak," they called me, roaring with laughter. When the grown-ups came back for me, they returned my sand molds right away. One of them chucked me under the chin and said, "How delicious!" But I couldn't make shapes in the sand anymore because we had to leave.

We also went for a walk on a little path. He was in his carriage and you couldn't even see his face. I walked behind with my beach toys in a little suitcase, but there was no sand there, and we wouldn't have stopped anyway because we were going for a walk.

The next day they left me on the sand again with the other kids. "Hi, Miss Kodak," they said to me. "Bring your sand molds?" I was afraid they would lose them, so I watched to see where they were taking them, until the grown-ups came back to pick me up.

The following day I said I didn't want to go to the beach because the other kids took my molds. They replied, "Nice little girls lend their toys," and they left me on the beach.

I sat with my legs together, but they never called me by my real name, nor did anyone ever try to find out what it was. "Here comes Miss Kodak," they said.

I never got to play with my sand molds, even though they were never lost. When the grown-ups came back, the kids would return them to me, I'd put them in the little suitcase, and off we'd go to our hotel.

Photos of this period? Yes, we have several: of them standing behind the baby carriage, of him in the carriage, wearing a beret to protect him from the sun, and of me, off to one side with my little suitcase full of sand toys. And no, you can't see my panties.

SINCE I ALREADY KNEW HOW TO READ AND WRITE, I SPENT a great deal of time sitting at my desk, doing nothing. The top of the desk was too slanty, and my pencil would roll to the floor every few minutes. The teacher was scary: she was taller than the blackboard. She was so scary that one little girl shit her pants in class.

"González," the teacher said, "come up here with your reader."

The González girl was skinny, with thick glasses, and she wore her hair pulled back tight and tied on top of her head with a bow. She stood in front of the class with her open book and said nothing.

"Read," the teacher said.

The González girl didn't read. She didn't even look at her book. She was looking at something at the back of the room. I don't know what she was looking at, because the teacher wouldn't let us turn around. Besides, we had to sit with our arms crossed, and it's hard to turn around in that position.

"Miss González, what's your problem?" the teacher went on. "Why aren't you reading?"

Then González, as pale as she was, turned all red and shit herself. She had diarrhea, so she spewed out streams of mustard-colored liquid shit everywhere, but she never let go of the book and she didn't stop staring at whatever it was at the back of the classroom. The teacher got up, grabbed her by the arm, and took her outside. Shortly afterwards, don Miguel came in with his bucket and mop.

Since I entered the class in midyear, they called me "the new girl." Besides being new, I was short, so I became a sort of mascot. Apparently I didn't like this, judging by my expression in the picture they took in the schoolyard at the end of the school year. The only class I liked was music. We used to get together in groups of four at the back of the music room, with the windows and doors closed in order not to disturb the rest of the school. Since the room was airless, one time a girl became violently ill, and while we were intoning "Glorious ensign of my fatherland," she leaned forward and threw up on the back of my neck.

Don Manuel had to escort me home at ten in the morning, which made me furious, especially since it wasn't even my fault.

WHENEVER I WATCHED THEM WALKING ARM IN ARM across the schoolyard, talking quietly, I thought of them as grown women, with tits, hips, and waistlines. We were talking about the punctured Host. I was half listening and half watching them. They hardly even looked at me. Occasionally they would bend down from their great height, chuck me under the chin and say, "Look how cute." Then we resumed our discussion of the punctured Host.

At each side of the main altar there was a door through which the priests who said Mass and the altar boys would enter. Where did those doors lead to? To the country? No, not to the country. They led to a half-empty room, with a dough-kneading table in the middle and an oven off to onc side.

They kept on walking by in two's and three's, talking about mysterious things.

Before throwing away a piece of bread, I kiss it four times, making the sign of the Cross. Because the bread is the Body of God. Any kind of bread: a Host, a French bread, a baguette, a hamburger bun, a peasant loaf, a pumpernickel. So you mustn't throw the bread away without kissing it, because if you do, God will punish you. Now let's talk about the punctured Host.

They're huge, oppressive, suffocating. Their bodies eclipse the horizon. When they surround me, I can't see past them; I can't find my classroom or the principal's office or the water fountain.

The boy entered the half-empty room behind the main altar. He didn't have permission but he did it anyway because the devil tempted him. The devil told him: "Go in and see what the Host is like, that thing you swallow without chewing or even looking at it." The boy knew he mustn't be curious, because curiosity is a sin.

"How would it be if we dressed her all in black? For the scene of colonial Buenos Aires?" asked the fourth-grade substitute, who was the same height as the sixth-graders. "Perfect," said the music instructor as she chucked me under the chin. Once again they planned to paint my face with burnt cork. Now let's get back to the punctured Host.

The boy entered the room with a pin in his hand, and he went straight to the table where the Hosts were for the following day's Mass. He grabbed one and stuck it several times with the pin. He stuck it several times! And the room filled up with blood. Because the Host is the Body of Our Lord, and anyone who plans to stick it had better know how to swim, or he'll drown in the blood of Our Lord Jesus Christ, amen. Don't throw away bread without kissing it first.

And why would he want to stick the Host? How should I know? What I want to know is, how could so much blood come out of a single Host? Which just proves that God can do anything. It was liquid, red blood. And then did he leave? What did they do with all the blood of Our Lord? Be quiet, child, the bell's rung. The fourth-grade teacher fought with the lower-school teacher and grabbed her by the hair. How could that be, if the lower-school teacher wears her hair really short, in a boy-cut, and smooths it down with Brilliantine? The fourth grade teacher fucks the porter. Fucks? What's that? She doesn't know! She doesn't know what that is! Where did the blood go? And why would he want to stick a pin in the Host?

No one ever really knew why Mele didn't work. She was always that young, single woman who painted and never earned a cent. A long-ago boyfriend dumped her, and she didn't recover from the disappointment for quite a while. She practiced fencing in a neighborhood club. The other fencers didn't pay much attention to her once the matches were over. Mele would hang up her foil, her chest protector, and her mask in the locker, and she'd go off and socialize with the club librarians, two skeletal, bespectacled women who were very, very nice. Men hardly ever came into the library. Only the pianist who accompanied the gymnastics classes, always with the same music (the waltz "Tears and Smiles," executed with different rhythms to suit the rhythm of the exercises), and occasionally a pimply adolescent who was in the process of reading all the novels of Emile Zola. The librarians diligently looked for something that would be appropriate for my age, but they found only one thing: the biography of Erasmus of Rotterdam.

After spending years at the club with no results, and fearing that she might become an old maid, Mele bought herself a knitting machine. It was an enormous device, very ugly and hard to operate. She managed to extract three garments from it, one in burgundy, one carrot-colored, and another in bottle green. In those days no one was wearing bright colors at our house: we were in mourning for Papa's death. The garments were donated to some people who let us use their house in the country for our vacation.

The country of which I'm speaking is an indefinite place, somewhere near La Pampa province. After an interminable trip, the train left us in a desolate town, where a man waited for us with a horse and buggy (the man, the buggy, and the horse were all very old). He took us, amid a cloud of dust, to the asshole of the world.

The owner of the house was another of Amanda's sisters-in-law. She didn't pronounce her *l*'s or *r*'s or, in fact, any other sound, in a distinctive way. She simply didn't talk. She worked like a mule all day long, assisted by her four blonde, sullen daughters. Every morning they shook out the goosedown quilts (imported from Russia) until they were nice and fluffy, so that it was a pleasure to dive into them head first. The walls were covered with an incredible number of flies. But as soon as you stepped outside the door, the flies ended and the countryside began. Chickens here, pigs there. Don Moishe planting corn on the right side, and the little farmhand scratching himself on the left. The boy was useless, but he had been brought up in the house and was like a member of the family.

The closest neighbor lived about twenty blocks away. Once in a while we would take the sulky to go visit him. After the first visit, I said I didn't want to go back, because they also had chickens, pigs, flies, goosedown quilts, and sullen children who didn't want to play. But they would never leave me alone in the house with the little farmhand because Mama said it might be dangerous. So I had to suffer through the visits. Since it was the dry season, all they talked about was the drought, of how it didn't rain, of how people and animals were suffering, and how sad it all was, dammit.

Everyone went to bed at siesta time, but they couldn't force me. I stepped out into the countryside beneath a punishing sun. I would pick up little chicks and ducklings, squeeze them a bit, and drop them from a certain height. Usually they survived, but some of them ended up slightly dopey, or else they walked crooked. If they ever did reach adulthood, they might have turned out to be defective chickens and ducks. I never had a chance to find out, because after a month we returned to Buenos Aires. As Mele used to say, out of sight, out of mind. Those of you who feel sorry for the animals can look for the beam in your own eyes.

I went over to the pigpen. I watched the pigs roll around in the mud and I threw them yellow ears of corn that I pulled out of a trough. There were never enough for them. If some of them got hit in the head, it was no accident.

The bathroom was near the pigpen. It was impossible to differentiate the stench of the pig sty from that of the cesspool. Squatting over the hole on the wooden plank, one had deep thoughts: the depth of the cesspool, its terrible contents, stories of children who had fallen into the hole, the pigs, the country, the dangerous hired hand.

The trip back home always seemed longer than the one going. We had to change trains in Carhuá. As there was an hour's wait, we went for a walk around the city. It was two in the afternoon: the streets were deserted and the stores were closed. We stopped to look at faded candies and ancient pastries in the window of a bakery called "Truth." Then we returned to the station to wait for the train. Time started up again, although very, very slowly, with the first howls of the approaching locomotive.

BECAUSE OF THEIR INFERIOR SITUATION AS RELATIVES-in-law, Papa's brothers were looked down upon by the Beasts. While Papa was alive, all this scorn was concealed beneath a thin cloak of courtesy, conversations about lost oxen, and a plethora of apologies and explanations for all sorts of idiocy. After his death, the relationship between the two families became very strained. As usual, the sharpest barbs were exchanged among the women. The men kept themselves somewhat removed, smiling.

One of Papa's brothers was nice. They called him Tártaro. Like the asthmatic brother, Tártaro sold clothing door to door, on the installment plan. He gave me my entire Jules Verne collection. He had a soft, reedy laugh. He found everything amusing, even sad things that no one finds amusing.

Another one of Papa's brothers was intelligent. He used the dictionary all the time, made predictions about the future of Europe, and no one in the family made any financial decisions without consulting him. His wife was blonde (yeah, right, bleached blonde, according to the Beasts), and she kept a set of beribboned perfumed bottles on her dresser. She wore a lot of makeup (yeah, pure whitewash). She was so polite that she herself would finish other people's sentences, to save them the trouble. She would wait with her mouth open until the other person reached the middle of the sentence, and then she would finish it however she saw fit, so enthusiastically that no one corrected her even if her version didn't coincide with the speaker's intention. Her house had a happy, somewhat chaotic atmosphere. Her little boy always had a cold and seemed to be addicted to nose drops. He wouldn't let anyone touch his collection of little nose drop bottles, and the odor of mentholatum floated in the air in his room.

Still another one of Papa's brothers was short. He had already received his certification as a notary, and he was engaged to be married to a fat woman who wore sky-blue crepe dresses. But Uncle Shorty was the youngest in the family, and his brothers still pinched his cheeks by way of greeting, popped candies into his mouth, and reminded him to pee before he went out, so he wouldn't need to go in the middle of the street. My librarian aunt used to sit him on her knees and bounce him up and down, saying "Giddy-up horsie!" This would make everyone except Uncle Shorty's fiancée die laughing. The aunt with liver disease would grab her liver with both hands, the asthmatic uncle would go to the bathroom, choking, the intelligent uncle would look up definitions in the dictionary, the bleached-blonde aunt would finish up everyone else's laughter and administer nose drops to her little boy. Uncle Shorty's fiancée made plans to move with him to Australia. And everything was happiness, peace, and joy.

After the obligatory engagement period, Uncle Shorty married his fat fiancée. In accordance with the custom of that time, he had to deflower her on their wedding night, in a room in the hotel. According to my classmates' explanation, as soon as the newlyweds arrived at their hotel room, the bride would lock herself in the bathroom, get undressed, and put on a nightgown that had been specifically chosen for the occasion. Meanwhile, the groom would undress, as quickly as possible, and slip into his pajamas, so that the bride, on emerging from the bathroom, would not find him naked.

As soon as he saw her, the groom would shed his customary shyness and courtesy and turn into a real animal: he'd rip off his pajamas, tear off her nightgown, throw her on the bed and hurl himself on top of her, foaming at the mouth. The victim would emit heart-rending shrieks, and a lot of blood would be spilled. The next morning they would have to get rid of the sheets and the mattress in order to avoid any embarrassment with the maids.

Before marriage, no woman with half a brain would ever let her boyfriend do anything to her. Anyone who did, according to the Beasts, was stupid, because she'd lost the only thing that men valued in a woman: her cherry. Any stupid girl who let him pluck it prematurely ended up scorned and abandoned, and she'd have no choice but to become a whore.

In order to illustrate these concepts, when I became old enough, my mother gave me a well-nourished bibliography of books that had been in vogue during her own youth, at the dawn of sex education. One of them said:

> *In men, the exercise of sexual function is reduced to the satisfaction of an organic need, revealed by the urgent demands of procreative desire, with their concomitant passions, and to a complex phenomenon of secretions and excretions that take place under special circumstances. In women, emotion is stronger than reproductive instinct, love more powerful than desire; man makes the overtures, and woman accepts (yeah, right, if she's stupid, say the Beasts). In women, dreams of married life and the inherent joys of motherhood are predominant.*
>
> Dr. Francisco Otero, *General Hygiene*
> Buenos Aires, 1919

According to the Beasts, there were certain women who actually liked it. They were as crazy as bedbugs. They went after men regardless of their marital status, and they were a constant danger to decent homes. Among those women who had "nothing to lose" were: actresses, dancers, nurses, maids, and postal workers. Decent women included: teachers, pharmacists, librarians, and married women without children, with certain rare exceptions, of course.

With regard to other prematrimonial expressions of affection, there were some lovely advice columns written by a progressive priest, less theoretical than Dr. Otero's recommendations. They were in dialogue form:

Question: May a girl kiss her boyfriend?
Answer: She may.
Question: May she give him a rather long kiss?
Answer: She may. What she may not do is keep on kissing him and kissing him, or caressing and embracing him, because that is a preamble to other activities that come later, with marriage.

Catholics like this author, scientists like Dr. Otero, traditional Jews like Papa's siblings, half-renegade Jews like the Beasts—they all agreed on a single point: you'd better watch out for your cherry. In general and in particular, there was no need to be stupid, right?

After you were married you could do anything you wanted, including seeking pleasure, according to the instructions in the manual *The Perfect Marriage*. Every so often it was emphasized that these instructions were for legally married couples: "The husband should massage his wife's clitoris," et cetera.

THE SUMMER AFTER PAPA'S DEATH, WE WENT QUITE often to the house in Saavedra. We sat on the porch and drank musk rose syrup with seltzer. Each time, Grandma Ana looked paler and more worn out. Between my comings and goings to and from the weed patch, I overheard snatches of sad conversations. "Impossible," Grandma Ana said. "In something, you have to believe in something." "All right, all right," Mama said. "I shouldn't have mentioned it to you."

But she *had* said it. She had said that Papa wasn't anywhere, that the dead aren't anywhere. Only old people and children are capable of believing that they're on a star, or some foolishness like that. Everyone remained silent, avoiding each other's eyes. One of the uncles noticed that I was standing there, hugging a column of the porch, and he took me by the hand and led me to the desk, a place where I generally wasn't allowed to go. He sat me in the revolving chair and opened a drawer so I could take out whatever I wanted.

I had a treasure chest at my disposal: pencils, pens, erasers, penknives, blotters, paperweights, unused keys, rubber stamps. I pressed one into the ink blotter and then onto a piece of paper. It said:

DO NOT DISTURB

I stamped it several times. When they came to get me, the stars were already out. From the garden next door came the scent of jasmines. In the Saavedra house, as in the house in Donato Alvarez, all fragrances came from the garden next door.

After Papa's death, Otilia, Clark Gable, and the Chipmunk came to live at our house. The Chipmunk was already two or three years old. He raced up and down the patio incessantly on his hobby horse. He ate plaster off the walls and dirt from the flowerpots. My brother, who was a little older, taught him the mysteries of life. The two of them used to sit on the patio and talk for hours. One day they were discussing hitting people in the head with sticks, of what happens to someone who's hit in the head with a stick.

"He gets quiet. He passes out," my brother said.

"What does that mean, 'passes out'?" the Chipmunk inquired.

My brother assumed a professorial air. "Passed out means quiet, lying on the ground with your eyes closed, like sleeping. You can't see, you can't hear. You don't know what's going on."

The Chipmunk listened with concentration while he dug a hole in the wall where he extracted his plaster.

At the other end of the patio, I was descending into the crater of an extinct volcano with Jules Verne's expedition. Grandma peeked out to take a look, saw that all was calm, and went back into the kitchen to cook one of her concoctions. At the very moment we spied the shadow of the mysterious underground creature, I suddenly felt the roof cave in on my head. I didn't quite pass out, but nearly. Standing in front of me and staring at me intently was the Chipmunk, with a stick in his hand.

He was disappointed. Not only did he not get to see how someone passed out, but he had to spend all day in his room so no one else would knock him unconscious.

During all this, Otilia's belly grew bigger and bigger. I overheard snippets of conversations that eliminated all doubt. During Otilia's pregnancy, her fights with Mama got worse. Mama added a new insult to the usual litany: cow. But Otilia wasn't a peaceful cow, like the one that appeared every so often in the middle of *Billiken*, with her calf by her side and a border of cheese, butter, cream, and other dairy products all around her. She was a wild cow, with hyena eyes and the tongue of a poisonous snake.

I saw the Chipmunk's baby sister in a room in Rawson Hospital, where two rows of beds were lined up, stretching all the way to forever. He was in a crib that was covered with netting, at the foot of Otilia's bed. At the foot of each bed there was a crib. Otilia pointed out one that was empty. The baby had been born dead. The mother was half sitting up, her head propped up by her elbow, looking all around, slowly.

A few days later Otilia came home with the baby. As it was so hot, they left her outside on the patio in her little carriage. I took it upon myself to protect her from being hit by a ball and from the boys' experiments. I'd heard the Chipmunk ask my brother what would happen if they put her on the ground and tried to make her walk.

Living together became truly terrible. Chaos, fighting, the heat, the baby's crying, all conspired to turn the house into a living hell. Clark Gable, without ever losing his good humor, dug in his heels to try to improve the family's financial situation. One day they all left: Otilia, Clark Gable, and the two children. When the noise and ruckus finally quieted down, we could see just how decrepit and abandoned the house really was.

"ACT DUMB," OTILIA ADVISED ME. "CHANGE THE SUBject." To help me understand what she meant, she illustrated by relating a conversation she had had with a neighbor. It was December, when a great deal of activity was going on in preparation for the approaching holidays.

"You have to do your shopping early," the neighbor remarked, "because at the last minute it's always a madhouse."

"I know," Otilia replied, already on guard.

The neighbor blurted out, "Do you people celebrate Christmas?"

"No," said Otilia.

"What religion are you?"

"We aren't religious," Otilia said, since she was no dummy.

"But your parents, your grandparents, what religion were they?"

Otilia decided to cut her short: "They weren't. They weren't any religion. Look, excuse me, but I've got something burning in the oven." And she left her standing there.

This attitude didn't coincide with that of my paternal aunts, who said that I should never hide my Jewishness from anyone, and furthermore, that I should advertise it all the time by wearing a little chain with the Star of David around my neck.

This was a conflict for me. During a lecture about Christians and Jews, my fifth grade teacher asked all the Jewish girls in the class to raise their hands. A few did, as meekly as when she would ask those who had finished solving a math problem to raise their hands. My own two hands remained on my desk top. On the back of my neck I felt the outraged breath of my Grandma Ana, of my great-grandmother, and of King David himself, as well as that of my Jewish classmates, who were clever at guessing your origin from your surname. But I also felt the approving looks of the Beasts. I was learning not to be a dummy by playing dumb.

Once the teacher had finished scrutinizing the faces of those who had raised their hands, she gave them permission to put them down again and continued with her explanation. She said that the Jews were still paying for a crime that they had committed two thousand years ago: killing Jesus Christ. The proof of this was the fact that so many Jews had died in the war (Poor things! she added). Their punishment would end when all the Jews converted to Christianity and accepted Jesus, who, she said, was infinitely merciful. At this point the bell rang and we went out to recess, although not before the teacher could pass around the charity collection box.

After they married traditional Jews, the Beasts changed their philosophical orientation. They ended up becoming bastions of Jewish pride, and as their financial situation improved, they became involved in social and recreational affairs and charity events sponsored by the Jewish community, competing with the other ladies in the community in the areas of clothing, jewelry, home furnishings, dietitians, and summer vacations at the beach. "She has a Russian Jew face that makes you want to throw up," Otilia said, referring to one of them. "But she's invited me to her house lots of times, so tonight I'm inviting them. No sense in being stupid," she pronounced. "It's best to hang around with members of the community. When they talk about you, at least they won't say, 'She has a Russian Jew face that makes you want to throw up.'"

Mama said that she, the Beasts, and Grandma were going to end up in the insane asylum. Mama shouted this from the middle of the patio, grabbing her head with both hands. Mele seconded this: Yes, they would all end up in the insane asylum. There, each one would go her own way, without recognizing the others, gesticulating and talking to herself, eternally rehashing the same old fight.

Suddenly I realized that I was alone on the patio. Through the Venetian blinds, I could see Mama and Mele in their rooms. Clad in faded bathrobes, they had thrown themselves on their beds and were staring up at the ceiling.

The front doorbell rang. It was one of Mama's cousins who had dropped in for a visit. While Mama and Mele got dressed to greet her, I brought chairs out to the patio and made polite conversation.

Mama and Mele asked about all the Doras and Leons. The cousin asked if they knew what had happened to the daughter of Leon the Watchmaker. Silence. They looked at me and sent me to my room. Sitting on the floor next to the Venetian blind, I could overhear the conversation quite comfortably. Leon the Watchmaker's daughter had been committed to the insane asylum.

"Crazy?" Mele asked.

"Crazy," the cousin replied.

The details left no room for doubt: the girl had walked out naked into the street. A policeman stopped her, and the end of the story is that they had her committed.

This calmed me. The real crazy woman was locked up. Mama and Mele discussed the matter with their cousin with the shocked and sorrowful tone one uses for those things that don't affect one personally. While I waited for permission to return to the patio, I thought: "Crazy. The daughter of Leon the Watchmaker went crazy. She ran out naked into the street. That's what a real crazy person is like."

To all the clubs and loyal fans
Who gather by our side
The Football League, the Football League
Salutes you all with pride.

All of us were from Boca. After the radio program "The Championship," when everyone was taking a siesta and Clark Gable was listening to the game, I shut myself up in the living room, the only decent room in the house, with a large window facing the street. In there was Papa's only legacy: his bookcase.

One of the three glass doors of the bookcase was locked with a key, because that's where the forbidden books were kept. I could take them out quite easily by sticking my arm in through the side door, since there were no separations between the three sections of the bookcase. One of the books was *Love Letters* by Marcelo Peyret. It narrates, through letters, the love affair of a guy, Marcelo, with a young lady, Beatriz. He desperately wants her to have intimate relations with him before marriage. She becomes angry and resists, though not for lack of desire, as she confesses to a close friend in a letter. As Ramiro keeps insisting and Beatriz is nobody's fool, she breaks off the relationship and marries another suitor, a dolt, but a dolt who respects her. With all this going on, and always strictly through correspondence, Beatriz's husband is insulted by Ramiro and has a duel with him.

Ramiro is gravely wounded. This stokes Beatriz's passion for him, and she decides to go see him (since she'd lost her cherry anyway, no one would notice if anything happened between them). She approaches his sickbed, dressed only in a peignoir. But he smiles sadly and says that "he (Ramiro) is no longer a real man." At the end, everyone commits suicide, except for Beatriz's close friend, who collects all the letters and sends them to Monsieur Marcelo Peyret so he can write this book.

In order to get into the last drawer of the desk, which was also locked with a key, I used a technique similar to the one for the bookcase: I pulled out the drawer above it, and voilà: all the forbidden items were at my disposal. I saw my parents' marriage documents, where my birth and my brother's were recorded, as well as my father's death, along with the funeral notice and some obituary notes from the newspaper. They said that the teaching profession had lost an educator, and the world of letters had lost a poet.

Similar sentiments appear on his tombstone, engraved on a bronze plaque in the form of an open book. Upon the marble rectangle that marks the place where he is buried, there is a single, not very legible inscription in square, unraised letters. It says, "Daddy."

I'M AWAKENED BY A KNOCKING AT THE DOOR THAT connects our room with the dining room. Mama suffers from insomnia; the knocking awakens her just minutes after she's finally managed to fall asleep. As I try to clear my head, I hear her let loose one curse after another. It's Grandma who is knocking, to let everyone know she doesn't feel good. She knocks with her open palm, because, as everybody knows, she's too weak to make a fist.

Mama shouts: "What do you want?"

No answer. I cover my head with the blanket. One second later the knocking begins again. Mama gets up so violently that I cover my ears. But instead of heading in the direction of the door where the knocking is coming from, she goes the opposite way, towards Mele's room.

"Get up and take care of your mother, bitch, or do you think I'm a slave to all of you?" Mama shouts. "I take care of her every night, you bitch, you viper. This time it's your turn."

Meanwhile the knocking continues at the dining room door. I get up and open the door. Grandma is standing a few steps away, next to the dining room table, supporting herself on it with both hands. She's trembling badly, regarding me with the eyes of a beheaded saint. While I accompany her back to her room, she leans on me with all her weight. Her hand is sweaty.

Dear little granny,
second mother of mine:
If only I could fly,

to the stars, all on high,
choose the brightest, choose the whitest,
choose the closest to the moon,
to adorn my granny's room.

Now I've got her tucked in bed, groaning rhythmically, while she gives me instructions for preparing her herb tea. In the distance I can still hear Mama and Mele fighting.

I return to the kitchen with the brew and a damp cloth, which Grandma puts on the back of her neck. Every five minutes I have to refresh the cloth under the bathroom faucet. Then I ask, "How do you feel, Grandma?" "The same, child, the same," she groans.

"But what's the matter with you, Grandma?"

"I'm very weak, child."

"What a repulsive face you have, Grandma!"

"The better to frighten you, Little Red Riding Hood."

"What trembly hands you have, Grandma!"

"The better to rip you apart, Little Red Riding Hood."

"What disgusting concoctions you drink, Grandma!"

"They're to make me immortal, Little Red."

Could've been worse. Because I was afraid Grandma was going to die. That, I couldn't tolerate. Couldn't tolerate it? I begin to think about Grandma's death. There she is in that bed, dead. With the wet cloth on the back of her neck, the steaming tea, exuding its foul odor, her false teeth in the glass of water. Mama and Mele have called a moratorium and are at the bedside, all bug-eyed and holding their hands to their mouths. Otilia arrives, screams, covers her mouth with her hand, and goes all bug-eyed as she looks at Grandma. A train brings Amanda from General Pico, so she, too, can shout, cover her mouth with her hand and bug her eyes at the bedside of her dead mother. More people arrive to see Grandma. They all comment on how lifelike she looks. Tomorrow I can skip school. The teacher will point to my empty desk and say, "The Steimberg girl is absent because her grandma died." A silence will follow, and then two kids will burst out crying, one because his grandma already died, and the other because his might. The teacher will suggest that all the children who are lucky enough to still have their grandmas should pray for them and behave nicely, so their grandmas will live many more years.

I haven't heard her groan for a while now; she's completely still. I jump out of my chair and go to the head of the bed. Her watery eyes flutter beneath the wet cloth. The hand that is resting on the comforter trembles slightly.

"Do you feel better, Grandma?"

Dear little Granny,
second mother of mine.

Laziness: synonym of sloth or idleness. Characterized by a natural aversion to work, which, if taken to an extreme, gives rise to all the physical and moral defects associated with inactivity.

Dr. Francisco Otero, *General Hygiene*,
Chapter 19: "The Hygiene of Passion"

In the woods, in China,
a Chinese girl got lost,
and as I also was alone,
her path and my path crossed.
It was n-i-i-i-ght time
and the little Chinese gi-i-i-i-rl...

Feliciano Brunelli, Juan Carlos Barbaró, and their traditional orchestras. I move the dial:

Midnight Mass,
I'm no longer the man I once was...

I want to get married in white, in a haze of chiffon and orange blossoms, and I want them to play Schubert's Ave Maria during the ceremony. That's why I have to find myself a Catholic boyfriend and convert to Catholicism. There's no rush: I don't plan to get married before I'm eighteen, and now I'm twelve.

In order to convert to Catholicism, you have to believe in Jesus Christ. That's very simple: how can you not believe in someone who's right there, hanging over the doorframe? He's got a beard, he's smiling, and he's wearing a white tunic and is surrounded by a fluffy golden cloud. With his right hand he makes a sign: *V* for victory. Jesus is calling me; he touches my face. Jesus sees me. I run my hands over my body. Holy water washes away all sins, all of them. Whoosh! In the place where Jesus was, now Frank Sinatra is standing.

Strangers in the night...

But anyway, with holy water...whoosh! No more Jesus, no more Frank Sinatra. Now it's Mama standing in the doorway. Silence and horror.

Several hours after seeing these apparitions, I found the following message stuck between the pages of my Student Manual:

Alicia:

Today when I got home, exhausted from the sheer weight of all the responsibilities I must assume because of my situation as a widowed mother of two children, whom I have to support and educate, I was expecting to find you bent over your books (which I provide for you with so much effort), so that you will be able to fend for yourself someday. But imagine how hurt I was to discover you lying in bed, in a shameful position (which could cause irreparable damage to your spine), using your hands to do something that I don't even dare mention here, because it would make me die of despair and shame.

Think, Alicia, before it's too late, of the perversions and incurable illnesses your behavior might cause, and tell me if this is the reward I deserve, I, whose fate it is to live a life of continuous suffering and sacrifice so that my children may grow up to be healthy, worthwhile people. Don't forget that other women in my circumstances would lock their children up in boarding schools instead of sacrificing their own lives to bring them up properly.

Read and memorize the sections that I've marked in Dr. Otero's book, and then, if you still want to go on slowly killing yourself, and me too, with your behavior, go right ahead.

YOUR MOTHER

These are the sections that I found underlined in Dr. Otero's book:

Regarding Onanism: The most frequent abuse of pleasure among the younger generation is onanism or masturbation. Onanism cannot be considered a passion, because passions always have a noble cause which gives them an appearance of morality, through which the spirit finds, at heart, a tendency to goodness which makes them more or less agreeable to one's conscience. Everything about onanism, on the other hand, is degrading, since it possesses not even an ounce of delicate sentiment to mitigate its coarseness: everything is reduced to the desire to find pleasure in the act of wasting a treasure that is precious both to the individual and to the propagation of the species. It goes against Nature's Plan, which is to imbue these acts of propagation with pleasure, in order to irresistibly attract animals to validate this plan by perpetuating their species.

The principal causes of this aberration are: reading enervating novels; idleness and sloth; and, above all, cultivating friendships with others similarly affected by this vice. In general it is difficult to detect traces of this unfortunate habit, as masturbators always seek solitude to engage in their lewdness, and since their shame and confusion make them too timid to confess their errant ways.

Nevertheless, there are quite a few symptoms that invariably reveal the vice, no matter how shallowly rooted it may be: a pale face, bluish circles around the eyes, swollen, rheumy eyelids, discolored lips, faltering strength, unsteady gait, an air of diffidence before one's superiors, lack of vigor or desire to study, weakening memory. The imagi-

nation grows dull; moral tenor is lost, replaced by embarrassment or indifference. Life is viewed with disdain, and along with this listless physical and moral disorder, anguish and remorse exacerbate the suffering experienced in this very unpleasant state.

TÁRTARO, THE GOOD UNCLE, MARRIED CLOTILDE PÉREZ (Clota to her friends), a girl who wasn't from the Jewish community, but this didn't cause too much upheaval because Tártaro was one of the uncles few people noticed. Clota's mother was one of Tártaro's clients; every month Tártaro would stop by to collect his bill and sell her something else.

One day when it was raining really hard, Tártaro rang the bell and they invited him in for coffee. Sitting around the table were the owners of the house, and Clota. The rest was very simple.

You might say God rewarded Tártaro for his goodness. Not only did He give him a woman whose goodness was equal to his own, but He also willed him two made-in-heaven in-laws, people who were so kind that everything they touched turned to honey. True, there was a slight problem with flies, but the inconvenience was worth putting up with, if you considered that once you crossed the threshold of that house, all the evildoers in the world remained outside.

But the same God who rewarded Tártaro also sent him misfortune. One day, as usual, his mother-in-law was chasing the flies that were attracted to the house by the honey of her goodness, when she lost her balance and tumbled down the stairs. Tártaro found her unconscious at the foot of the staircase, and without knowing what else to do, he began to laugh.

Years later, with his soft, kindly laughter, Tártaro told me that since her accident the lady had never again gotten out of bed. Five years later, she died. “Thank God, that poor thing! It was a liberation for her and for us,” Tártaro said. “We took her” (Tártaro was becoming more and more animated) “to the cemetery in Azul, her home town. Shipping her there cost us a pretty penny, but how happy we are, knowing she’s finally where she always wanted to be!”

My asthmatic uncle came over nearly every morning to use our phone. He would bring me the comic section of *Crítica*. I had to thank him with a kiss, a real drag, because his cough disgusted me, and I still hadn't forgotten my leap into the smoldering ashes. But an uncle was an uncle, and comics were comics, so I gave him the kiss, which he returned accompanied with hugs and caresses.

He was a funny uncle, that one, with a strange way of being affectionate. His trembly fingers gave me goose flesh, when he touched me almost without touching me. I listened to his labored breathing as he caressed me, emitting a whistling noise from his chest. And those wild-eyed glances at the door! As soon as I could get away from him, I locked myself in my room and read the comics.

This happened many times, whenever he was alone with me, luring me with the comics that stuck out of his pockets. Finally, one day when I was tired of the comics and the pawing, I refused. He insisted, saying he was my uncle, and I had to be affectionate to my uncle. He was sitting next to the phone, and his fly was unbuttoned. "As usual," I thought. I was surprised to realize that this wasn't the first time I had noticed those unfastened buttons. We looked at each other for a moment, and then I left the room.

He never came by the house again. I would see him again during our occasional visits to Saavedra, but he didn't stay with us. He'd say hello and shut himself in his room, the windows and door firmly closed to keep out the pollen.

Grandma Ana died suddenly. As far as sickness was concerned, she had been sick since time immemorial. I never saw her as being any different from the way she was the day she died: wasted away, white hair, silent, with an expression of permanent pain. My uncles cried loudly, standing next to the bronze bed with little angels on the headboard. We all surrounded the bed, heads lowered. I didn't even think about the angel hair pasta in milk. They said that Grandma couldn't bear to observe the first anniversary of my father's death. Papa couldn't defend himself against these charges, so he was held responsible for her death, as well as having to bear the weight of his own.

That was a bad year for our family. Papa's older sister and Grandpa José died also. We had hardly gotten over one mourning period when we had to begin another, rigorously. My aunts were so overwrought that we had to visit them every Sunday. Luckily, no one was concerned about me, and so I had free access to the library. There wasn't too much to choose from, but there were a few titles with sinister appeal, like *King Hunger*, by Andreyev, which had the story of an attack on a couple in the woods and another about lepers; and yet another book of stories with one about a guy who finds a beggar woman in the street and brings her home to live with him. The beggar woman becomes pregnant, and with her pregnancy, she wastes away: she ends up walking on all fours, overcome by an unbearable weight. Then the guy leaves her, but later he feels sorry, so he comes back, but he finds her dead—dead!—in a pool of blood—blood!—and their baby has been born. He has no arms or legs and he's covered with hair. The man cries; he's the father of a monster. Finally he runs away and leaves the baby to drown in the pool of blood—ooh! blood! He lets him drown in blood, while he runs away, he runs away.

Come on, child, tea is served. Put down that book. The cups are on the tablecloth, your aunt with liver disease is at the head of the table, your grandparents are in their oval portraits on the wall, the mote is in someone else's eye, the baby's in a pool of blood, and here's the weekly death that leads to Monday.

María Belén taught me to pray. She was ten years older than I, had acne, and colored her lips dark red. She taught me the Our Father, the Hail Mary, the Credo, and another one which began: "Oh my God, I am heartily sorry..." Her job was to convert all the faithful on the block to Catholicism, especially the Japanese family from the dry cleaner's. The Japanese mother knew that her children were learning Christian doctrine, and all of a sudden María Belén took all seven of them to be baptized at once.

My conversion took place in secret. María Belén didn't dare mention it to my family, so we simply prayed together for a while every afternoon, looking at a different image for each prayer. We would install ourselves in the living room or the informal dining room, where I couldn't help fixing my glance on a glass container of water in which some mushrooms floated and expanded hideously, grown there by María Belén's grandmother for who knows what purpose. María Belén's grandmother, an ancient woman from Asturias, would come into the room to bring us sweet potato pastries and supervise what we were doing. If there was a storm, she'd come in and order us to lower our voices and stop praying: "Quiet, girls, it's the wrath of God!" she'd whisper, pointing heavenward.

Whenever the paperboy dropped off *La Razón*, María Belén's mother would put on her glasses and read the police reports aloud. She'd pay special attention to knifings and other violent crimes. One day an article came out that caused quite a stir: a woman had killed her husband by plunging a pair of scissors into his heart. María

Belén's mother dropped the paper and remained very quiet, with her mouth open, while the grandmother grabbed her head with both hands and exclaimed, "Oh my God, scissors are the worst weapon!"

After prayers, María Belén and I would practice drawing a man. I drew the hair, and she, the ears; she drew the torso, et cetera, until we finished the picture. We drew him naked and very hairy, with huge genitals in various stages of erection. If María Belén's mother or grandmother happened to come in, we'd hide the drawing under the Catechism and continue our discussion of Doctrine. Her grandmother looked at us approvingly: "Listen to María Belén, child; she'll teach you Doctrine very well. She also works very hard making Christians out of those Japanese children."

Only very important visitors were allowed into the formal dining room of that house: some priest or lawyer, perhaps. I only went in there once, very respectfully, to look at the family altar which María Belén's mother had installed. With the blinds closed, you could hardly make out the figure of Jesus on the wall, hanging above a little table that was covered with an embroidered cloth and little statues and crucifixes, as well as two big vases filled with tuberoses, carnations, and jonquils. Two constantly burning large candles illuminated the altar. María Belén's mother spent many long hours before that altar, as she was a proud, devout woman who didn't care to mix with the riffraff who went to church. "I deal with God in my own home," she declared, "and I never forget to provide Him with His candles or flowers. I'm sure those women who wiggle their butts coming out of Mass in their glad rags don't spend two hours a day on their knees before Our Lord, like I do."

In the bathroom of that house there were always wilted flowers. Peeing in that bathroom was like peeing in a funeral parlor. One of the bathroom doors connected to the bedroom where María Belén and her grandmother slept. One night, after peeing among the flowers, I went into the bedroom, turned on the light, and looked at myself in the wardrobe mirror. Something I saw in the reflection in the mirror chilled me: there was María Belén's grandmother in one of the beds, with a kind of white bandage wrapped around her head, staring at me from the depths of her sunken eyes, unmoving and silent. I ran to the door, turned off the light, excuse me, ma'am, I didn't know, and I bolted from the room, through the patio, and into the little informal dining room.

The man María Belén and I drew that night turned out remarkably well. He was dressed from the waist up, wore a short cape (Episcopal style, in an appropriate purple hue), and his head was draped in an Oriental turban, decorated with jewels and colored feathers. In one hand he held a sign that said, "DON'T BE AFRAID, GIRLS." His other hand held a tray that supported his enormous phallus. When it was done, we stuck it on the wall with a thumbtack, and we nearly exploded with laughter looking at it. Later on we tore it up meticulously into little pieces and flushed them down the toilet.

As I walked the few yards which separated María Belén's from mine, I silently repeated a new prayer she had taught me that evening.

CAROLINA LIVED ON THE OTHER CORNER. AT TWELVE she was already a grown girl who sat with her legs crossed, like a movie star. I, although the same age, still hadn't given up my little girl's clothing or habits. I did everything I could to imitate her, but it was hard for me. María Belén's mother and Carolina's mother were friends. Mama had nothing to do with them, or with any of the other women in the neighborhood.

Carolina's mother would drop by María Belén's house in the afternoon with her knitting, and the two ladies would sit by the window of the little informal dining room, always with the blinds closed. Whenever María Belén's mother heard footsteps on the path, she'd put her knitting aside and get up to look through the slats. If the person going by was someone from the neighborhood, she'd say, "hmm" as a sign of recognition.

"There goes that Japanese woman," she announced. "She's all puffed up again. When the husband comes back from Japan he's going to discover that his wife made three babies while he was away."

Carolina's mom looked up from her knitting with her mouth agape. "You mean the Japanese guy who lives with her isn't her husband? Well, anyway, all those Japanese look alike…"

It was at these afternoon sessions that I learned that the coal-seller's son-in-law was a bum and a womanizer; that one of the sons of the woman who owned the corner bar crawled into his mother's bed at night, even though he was already twenty years old; that José the greengrocer, after many years, had finally brought his girlfriend over from Italy and could hardly recognize her, she was so worn out and skinny; that the beautician's son turned out to be a Mongoloid because his mother never kept a promise she had made to the Virgin; that the Turks who owned the other store ate only raw meat; that the doctor's maid had undergone her second abortion in a year; that the seamstress's daughter went off to dances and left her poor mother bent over the sewing, spitting blood.

Carolina's mother never moved from her seat, because she was too fat to move quickly, but she listened to everything carefully and contributed with her own stories about other neighbors.

They never talked about themselves. They were decent housewives; nothing could ever happen to them. Actually, this was true. While María Belén went from being a girl to being a young lady, then a somewhat older young lady, and finally a rather oldish young lady, her mother never aged. She remained young and fierce, as she was when I met her, so that eventually she looked as young as her daughter, and finally, even younger. She never gave up her domestic devotion, changing the flowers and candles daily, just as she never gave up her evening reading of police reports, followed by the customary street inspection. When her mother and husband died in the same year, she made María Belén kneel before the dining room altar and vow that she would never leave her side. So María Belén grew old beside her young mother, but she went to bed with all the men on the block, married or single. Otilia, who became more tolerant later on, said, "Well, as long as she's never going to get married, let her at least enjoy herself, poor girl."

María Belén's mother had a fight with Carolina's mother, about whom she spread the rumor that she was crazy and under psychiatric care: she had gone out naked into the street, just like Leon the watchmaker's daughter. But they never put Carolina's mom in an insane asylum:

she had a doctor who treated her with pills. He didn't cure her altogether, but let's just say that she at least put a towel on when she went out into the street.

One fine day Mama forbade me to be María Belén's friend anymore. This happened because, after the argument with María Belén's mother, Carolina's mom came over and told Mama a few things that María Belén's mother had said about her: she said Mama was a stuck-up bitch who never mixed with any of the neighbors, and that her brothers-in-law (Papa's brothers) came over a bit too often (offering her own explanation about the reason for these visits).

But I missed María Belén, so I still saw her secretly from time to time. Once Mama caught me coming out of her house. She passed right by us without looking at us, her lips compressed, and she waited for me in the doorway of our house. I followed her inside, fearful of aggravating her further with any sign of renewed rebellion. All afternoon she didn't say a word to me. At night I found this message on my pillow:

Alicia:

I thought you understood why I didn't want you to have anything to do with María Belén and her family. It seems you don't understand a single word of insult directed against your mother, a word that should suffice for you to repudiate the person who pronounced it as well as anyone who goes near that person. My life is a constant sacrifice to give my children everything they need. Whatever I do, I do for the two of you, since my own life is forever ruined. But to think that someone should dare besmirch my name with the cesspool of her mouth, and that you, my daughter, with all that you owe me, should dare exchange a single word with that person, is more than I can bear. The only thing I can think is that you're just like her. If you continue to go to María Belén's house, it's because you too want to bury me in mud. And I wonder why, Alicia, why?

YOUR MOTHER

"GET OVER HERE."

"I didn't mean it."

"Get over here."

"I'm telling you I didn't mean it."

"Get over here if you don't want me to kill you."

"I wasn't thinking about what I was doing."

She twisted my arm while she shouted at me, but the pain was nothing compared to the terror of having her face so close to me, all tightened up, her teeth clenched.

As she twisted my arm, she interrogated me: "Why did you do it?"

"I didn't realize."

"You didn't realize!"

She let go of my arm just long enough to give me a smack that sent my head spinning.

"Listen to me, you filthy liar. No one does a thing like that without realizing it. Tell me why you did it."

"I was bored."

"Bored?"

She shoved me up against the wall. "So you were bored, huh?" (slap). "So while your mother is out struggling for your sake, you're bored?" (shove).

"I'm sorry."

"Bitch. Viper. This is what destiny has to offer me: a viper bitch who wants to destroy her mother."

She let go of my arm, which she had begun to twist again, and started to cry, covering her face with her hands. In the middle of her weeping, which I accompanied, she kept on complaining about her bad luck. After a while she left me alone, slamming the door on her way out.

I threw myself on the bed and cried for a long time. The slaps, as well as my irreparable material loss, really hurt. On the top part of the radio, a venerable RCA Victor that looked like a Gothic cathedral, was the figure of a woman, which I had carved with the point of a compass. It was a very ugly design, similar to dozens of others I executed on arbitrary pieces of paper, on the pages of my notebooks, and even in books. I wasn't concerned that the women come out beautiful, but I drew them with noticeable protuberances in the breast and buttocks areas. I never neglected to draw their cleavage peeking out of their low-cut, ruffled necklines. Mama had already scolded me for these semi-obscene sketches with which I wasted my time. But papers can be thrown away, and pages can be torn out of books and notebooks. On the other hand, the little woman carved into the radio couldn't be, would never be, erased.

Infractions like this one were destroying whatever remained of the loving relationship Mama and I once had. I became a habitual liar, lying even when it wasn't necessary. I lost and ruined countless belongings, I got incompletes in school, I fastened my torn bra straps with safety pins, I started associating with those girls Mama considered to be "dangerous," and I drew thousands of little women with huge butts and tits.

After those terrible beatings, I spent a long time wishing Mama dead. I would shake my fist at the door through which she had just exited, repeating, "I hope you die. I hate you. I hate you."

And then I began to recover. I washed my face with cold water and sat down to study. I would read two or three paragraphs, then stop for a moment to think about how I could reform, become good, honest, studious, and put an end to those horrible scenes with Mama. She would love me again, and I would go back to loving her. I was already beginning to love her, anticipating better times to come.

Secretly I would fulfill my wish to be baptized, and that would help me become a better person. Jesus, hanging once more above the door frame, smiled at me encouragingly. As always, he was dressed in white, had a lovely beard and a halo around his head. As always, he made a sign with his hands to communicate with me. But this sign was strange: I wondered what he could mean by that, digging his right index finger into the palm of his left hand and making screwing motions. When I finally understood, I turned bright red and returned my gaze to my book.

"Go on daydreaming and catching flies there with your mouth open" (that wasn't Jesus's voice; it was my mother's). "Go on catching flies with your mouth open while your mother sacrifices the last days of her youth so that you can study."

WHILE I FIGHT OFF WINTER WITH BLANKETS, HOT water bottles at my feet, and the sound of Bing Crosby on the radio, she goes through my room putting things in order.

"How sloppy you are, Alicia! You're disgusting!" She's found the safety pins with which I fasten bra straps, garters, belts. Among my clothing there are quite a few visible pins, like on the bald head in the Geniol headache remedy ad. My grandmother also occasionally leaves pins in the clothes she's fixed for me, and when I try them on, I never escape being stuck. They have to alter the hand-me-down dresses sent by Cousin Dora from Mendoza (who has a daughter my age) to fit my body. "Whenever you have clothing to throw away or give away, Doriucha, send it to Buenos Aires, because we're going through some hard times here," Mele had written her. And Doriucha replied with the first donation. "Hey, look, how elegant!" the Beasts remarked, distributing the clothing Doriucha and her daughter had sent. All of it had hardly been worn, but it was somewhat out of style.

Sometimes you have to remind rich people to remember the poor, or rather, those who are going through hard times. Truth is, we were rich people who were just going through hard times. Once they blew over, we would go back to our real station in life, similar to Doriucha's, with a fancy house, a chauffeured automobile, and a German nanny for the kids.

When Mele sent the letter to Mendoza, our side of the family had been going through hard times for about fifty years, a situation which started when my great-grandmother and her children had to escape from Russia with only the clothes on their backs. The most material comfort I ever experienced was during my early years, before my father's death. If he had lived, we wouldn't have endured the humiliation of having to ask our rich relatives to donate their used clothing to us, but instead we would have shit on them. Maybe we would have even sent them some little gift, to teach them a lesson. Not used clothes, because if you give it away it's just to avoid throwing it away, but nice gifts—the kind people buy on purpose specifically to give to someone.

But saying is one thing, and doing, another. When Otilia became a Rich Lady like Cousin Dora from Mendoza, she also began to play Lady Bountiful with her leftover old rags. But as she always wanted to make a good impression, instead of sending them to poor relatives, she donated them to the Israelite Home for the Aged. Otilia went from being as poor as a church mouse to being reasonably well-off but debt-free to being comfortable, and ultimately to becoming a bourgeoise pig, oink oink.

Then she started to make donations. Instinctively and unerringly she always sent them to the same place, thus earning herself a degree of prestige that was recognized in a letter sent to her from the Israelite Home. Otilia never missed an opportunity to talk about her donations and that letter.

"I give away a lot of clothes, all in very good condition. My daughters are so spoiled, they won't wear the same dress more than twice. The people at the Home are very grateful to me. They sent me A LETTER. You should see THE LETTER they sent me, it was so moving. I send the clothing there because you should take care of your own kind first. If one day you should need help, who do you think will give it to you? The people of the Jewish community! Sometimes I laugh," she added, "thinking how those little old ladies in the Home look in the girls' bikinis and jeans! But when I make up a package, I put in everything that's left over, so I can straighten up the closets while I'm at it."

And Otilia, with a virtuous expression, went off to sample a new recipe for a shake. She was one of the first ladies in Buenos Aires to have a television and a blender.

"Don't expect anything from anybody. No one is going to do anything for you. The only one who worries about you is your mother. Your mother, who suffered giving birth to you, who spent sleepless nights watching over you when you were sick, who deprived herself of everything to give you what you needed."

"Friends, hah! What do your friends give you? When you need something, you have to ask your mother for it. Did any of your friends ever give you what your mother gives you? No. Do they feed when you're hungry? No. Take care of you when you're sick? No. Help you make a future for yourself? No. So just don't worry about them. Worry about your mother. Go on, keep sticking your finger up your nose till it twists up like a sweet potato. Here, take this. Take this money your mother earned by the sweat of her brow and go get me a package of roach killer from the grocery. This house is full of disgusting bugs. Go on, hurry up, do something for your mother instead of plastering your ear to that radio, listening to stuff that makes you sick in the head. Go on. The money. Your mother. Suffering. Roaches. Finger up your nose. Friends? Roaches. Sacrifice."

On the way to the grocery store where I was going to buy the roach killer there was a church. It was usually empty, but around six in the evening you'd see some hunched-up old ladies go inside with their rosaries. I entered, touched the font of holy water, made the sign of the Cross accompanied by a slight genuflection, and walked between the rows of pews with my eyes on the main altar.

Everything was clean and polished, and it smelled of incense. Three or four old ladies down on their knees were praying the rosary so quickly you couldn't even see their lips move. I knelt down, far away from them, and tried to remember all the prayers María Belén had taught me. I also tried to recall the Catechism questions, like "Who is God?" God is the more excellent and admirable Being that anyone can describe or imagine, infinitely good and powerful and this and that and the other thing, and then afterwards come the prayers, I believe in God the Father almighty, Creator of Heaven and Earth, that one I can never completely remember, Our Father Who Art in Heaven, that one I know like the back of my hand, Hail Mary, with that business of the fruit of Thy womb (that makes me think bad thoughts), and Oh My God I am heartily sorry for having offended Thee, with a little tap on your chest every time you say heartily sorry.

I must be possessed by the devil, because every time I say "I am heartily sorry," I think of him. I believe in the devil and in hell with hellfire and eternal torments and all the rest of it. If you die with even a single mortal sin, you go to hell. If you die and are truly sorry for all your sins, no matter how many there are, or how terrible they are, even if you've jerked off twenty times a day for your entire life, you go to heaven anyway.

Heaven is full of repentant, happy jerk-offs, all of them with their wings, white robes, and golden sandals. They all revolve around God the Father, who smiles at them and loves them as if they had never jerked off at all. They don't have the desire to jerk off anymore, and they couldn't even if they wanted to, because underneath their white robes there's nothing there.

All the old ladies have gone now, except one. I pick up the package of roach killer that I had placed in front of me on the prie-dieu so I wouldn't forget it. I walk towards the door, followed by the remaining old lady. We reach the font at the same time, and simultaneously genuflect, making the sign of the Cross. I look towards the altar; the old lady looks at me. We walk outside. The old lady comes towards me: she wants to tell me something.

"Listen, child, in church you need to cover your head."

"Yes, ma'am, I know, but I didn't really plan on going to church. I was just passing by and I went inside."

"Listen, child, it doesn't matter to me. It's for God's sake. It's out of respect for God."

"Yes, ma'am, you're right. Next time I'll put my kerchief in my purse so I'll have it handy. It's just that, you know? I needed to go inside."

I suddenly notice that I'm crying, tears of rage.

I get out of there quickly, squeezing the package of roach killer as if it were the old lady's throat. Dried up old bitch, what do you know about my respect for God? All the old ladies in the world can go straight to hell.

"Why're you so late? Did you meet up with one of your disgusting girlfriends? And what about your mother? That's not the roach killer I told you to buy. Go back there right now and exchange it. Go on, just keep on wasting time like that! Forget about all my sacrifices. Forget about the roaches invading the house. Forget about your mother."

How lovely! Back on the street again. All the lights are on now. Dinner odors waft from all the houses. Jasmine is blooming in all the gardens. How lovely the street is, dear God!

I FELL IN LOVE WITH PAQUÍN, WHO HAD GREEN EYES AND played the guitar better than I did. He was the star of the Spadavecchia Conservatory's annual recital, playing a guitar and mandolin duet with his younger sister. Paquín's sister played the mandolin and was always the featured mandolin player at all the Spadavecchia concerts.

Every Tuesday and Friday I walked to the Conservatory with my sight-reading manual and my Williams's *Theory* book under my arm, lost in a fantasy in which I was grown up, beautiful, married to Paquín and triumphantly touring the world with him, playing guitar duets. The fantasies would dissolve as soon as I reached the door of the Conservatory and sat down in the hallway opposite a huge Venetian mirror, or Renaissance style, or whatever it was. In any case, it reached the ceiling. The walls were covered with pictures, some of them quite old, of Maestro Spadavecchia's performances with his students. There were several pictures of the nephew of Celeste Aída, the sight-reading teacher, when the boy was only four or five and already clutching a violin in his fist. He was dressed as a cossack (a Russian cossack, they would explain whenever they showed the photo). Others showed Spadavecchia's famous fifty-guitar orchestra. I played in that strange orchestra a few times. Fifty Conservatory students, undifferentiated by age or sex, would sit in a wide semicircle on the stage of some theater that had been rented for the occasion, with their left feet resting on little benches, and their sweaty fingers positioned to interpret whichever piece was on the program ("Arabian Capriccio" by Tárrega; "A Tear" by Sagreras, and other compositions of similar style, virtuoso pieces characterized by their great technical difficulty but which we bravely attacked nonetheless, to the great admiration of parents, other relatives and friends). When the curtain rose, all fifty performers felt chills up and down their spines.

After each piece there would be loud applause and cheering. At the end of the concert, right on the stage, there would be a celebratory lunch for students and parents. The concerts were given at the end of the year, when it was very hot, so taffeta and organdy dresses were de rigueur, the sandwiches spoiled and the orangeade lukewarm. There were also cream puffs that nobody tasted for fear of food poisoning.

Final exams followed the concert. Spadavecchia Conservatory was seized by a wave of hysteria. Far from calming the students down, parents and teachers alike terrified them as much as possible. Doors stood wide open because of the heat, so that from the hallway one could see Maestro Spadavecchia presiding over the guitar lessons, *mate* in hand.

The Maestro sucked away zealously, making loud noises with the straw as he reached the bottom, all the while tapping his foot in rhythm with the students' playing. When he had polished off his *mate* so thoroughly that the only thing left to suck up was the straw, he handed it over, without turning his head, to a squalid, worn-out creature who stood at his left, waiting humbly for Spadavecchia to stop sucking. This bit of human flotsam who ran back and forth all afternoon with the *mate* was the sister of Celeste Aída, the sight-reading teacher, and the mother of the precocious ex-Russian Cossack violinist. Before dismissing the student, the maestro would hand her the *mate*, take the guitar, and give a demonstration of how the selected piece should be played. The students got dizzy trying to follow his stubby, be-ringed fingers.

After exams during my final year at the Conservatory, there was a second, special concert, in which only the big shots participated: Spadavecchia, the piano, violin and mandolin instructors, and Aída Celeste's nephew. All the students were invited to attend. I didn't go, because the tickets weren't free. Consequently I missed my final chance to see Paquín and Maestro Spadavecchia. The maestro was standing at the top of a staircase in the theater during the intermission, when he rolled all the way down, felled by a heart attack. The second half of the concert was canceled, and an ambulance carried the maestro's body away. He died during intermission, so as not to interrupt the concert.

III

"FREEDOM! FREEDOM! FREEDOM!"

"Tamborini-Mosca, go with the flow!"

It was impressive to see all those people shouting, "Freedom! Freedom!"

Mama has a revolver. Cousin Quito came over to ask her for it, and she gave it to him so he could go out and fight for freedom and democracy.

Every time there was a serious blow-out at home Mama would say, "There's a gun in the house! I know where it is! I know, I know! I found it!"

She planned to kill herself with that gun. And what did your mother plan to do? Make stew for dinner? Well, mine planned to kill herself with that revolver!

"Your mother's dumb!"

"My mother is an important woman!"

Could she have forgotten that she gave the revolver to Quito? Could it be true she actually gave it to him? Was there only one revolver in the house, or were there two? Was there ever a revolver in the house? Could it be true that Papa had a revolver? Could Mama have been lying? She too?

"Perón won the election."

"It can't be."

"He won't last a month."

Ten years. He lasted ten years.

"We're democrats." How about you?"

"Death to Perón!"

"We read *La Nación* in my house. What about you?"

My mother carried *La Nación* under her arm, in plain view. And suddenly the city was filled with riffraff. That's what Perón did: he filled the city with riffraff. Those half-breed girls from the sticks put on such airs, as though they were princesses and not servants.

"Tamborini will be President; go with the flow!"

"Don't talk in front of the help; she might report you."

In my class only one girl is a Peronist. The rest of us are all democrats.

It was impressive to hear that crowd shouting, "Freedom! Freedom!"

Ten years. But afterwards, he really got crushed, that bastard. While he was getting crushed, we threw tomatoes at him. And the jokes we made at his expense!

"Tell me this country isn't rich; it's got everything."

"Were you there marching in the big demonstration, shouting, 'Freedom! Freedom!'? Didn't you see me there?"

"Did your old man and old lady tell you about the white berets the radicals wore? And the business about the bribes? Did they explain how those who came before Perón were sons of bitches too? About the Week of Tragedy? Did your grandmother tell you?"

"But now look what a mess we're in, with all those half-breeds in Buenos Aires. And that's not Uriburu's fault, or Yrigoyen's, either! It's Perón's fault, goddammit!

I wonder what became of the gun. But...was there really ever a gun?

"LADIES AND GENTLEMEN, I'VE GOT SHIVERS UP MY ASS."

When I was a little girl, my father said that to make me laugh. And you, what did your father do to make you laugh?

There's a photo of my dad on a platform, talking to some townspeople. My father was a radical. And yours?

He's talking to some people, a gathering of people. You never know what might happen when so many people are gathered together. Bomb attacks, police attacks. Someone might die in all the commotion. Better to watch from a balcony.

That's what my grandmother advised, whenever the police were mentioned. My grandfather taught her politics and gave her one daughter after another. Then he stopped talking to her about politics or anything else, and that was their form of birth control.

Mama was always interested in politics. She taught me who the good guys were and who were the sons of bitches. For instance:

1. Peronists are sons of bitches.
2. Anti-Peronists are sons of bitches, but they hide it.
3. All men are sons of bitches.
4. All women, including friends and relatives, are bitches, except Mama herself.
5. Children aren't sons of bitches.
6. My brother was a child.
7. I was already beginning to outgrow my childhood.

If there's anything Mama isn't guilty of, it's inconsistency. She adhered unwaveringly to the above-mentioned precepts her whole life long.

Grandma met Perón, and she began to grow senile only after Evita's time. During that portion of Perón's regime, she began to have difficulties eating because of her orthodoxy. Horse meat? Frozen meat? Two hours waiting in line for a block of butter? Before, on the other hand, there had always been plenty of butter. What has become of us, my God!

A plague on Perón. When they came to our school to choose a delegate for the High School Students' Union, we all agreed that each one of us would vote for herself, so no one would come out ahead and there would be no delegate. "This can't happen," said the chick from the High School Students' Union. "You'll have to vote again." We voted again, with the same results. Besides being anti-Peronists, none of us wanted to be in the HSSU because they said Perón took advantage of the girls in it and gave them cheap bracelets in return.

After the vote was taken, the sole Peronist girl in the class said to another one, "Vote for me." A third vote was taken, and she was elected delegate.

She wasn't the traitor; everyone knew she was a Peronist. The traitor was the girl who agreed to vote for her, don't you think?

Of course, you can't be a hero forever. Finally I too joined the Women's Peronist Party, out of fear. Or was it because in order to get your official papers you had to join? I really can't remember.

We shunned the girl who was elected delegate. Right away the order buzzed from ear to ear: "Don't talk to Pérez." She hung out by herself for a while, teary-eyed and blushing furiously. After a while, the girl who voted for her went over and started speaking to her. The next day, somehow or other, a few more girls approached her, and eventually all of us did.

"YOU SHITTY BASTARD, GIMME BUTTER!"

But the guy closed his doors because there was no more butter. That's just a manner of speaking, because when people say there's no more butter, there's always just a little bit more: for good customers, for the owner of the store, and for his family.

We had been waiting in line for two hours, and it was such a cold afternoon. It had even started to drizzle. The day before the owner of the dairy had said there would be butter.

At four he opened: by three o'clock the line was already a block long. All the scum of the neighborhood was there, including those people we didn't speak to. Some came with a kid, so they could get two blocks of butter—because the rule was one block per person. If some other woman in line didn't like you, she'd report you, and then all hell broke loose.

At exactly four o'clock the owner stepped outside, with a face that could sour milk, to look at all the people he had to sell butter to. Many of them weren't planning to buy anything else, and some weren't even his customers.

The weather was ugly, and the people had so much to do, which they couldn't do because they were waiting in line. Some mothers had left their little ones—or their sick relatives or their old folks—at home alone. Others were sick themselves: with rheumatism, allergies, sciatica, lumbago, high or low blood pressure. You heard all kinds of stories, every possible scenario.

The line began to push forward. Everyone started pressing up against the one in front of her, to keep people from cutting in. There's always someone brazen enough…"You, lady, get in back of the line. Can't you see there's a line? The line ends here. You, I'm talking to you. No, lady, I won't hold your place. I'm not holding anyone's place because then the ones in back will complain."

In front of me there are about fifty people. The first one in line is the pedicurist's son, the kid who has problems. He's not exactly a complete idiot, but he got sick when he was little, and he stayed strange. He's not altogether useless. He walks around the streets by himself, runs errands, understands what you tell him, as long as it's easy stuff, but he talks like he has marbles in his mouth.

When the dairy opened, he was the first one to go in. He came out with his block of butter in his hand and went running home. The line moved forward; the people kept going in and coming out with their butter. Suddenly it occurred to me to look behind me, and there he was again—the pedicurist's son. Many people were aware of it, but no one said anything. What could you say to a poor thing like that, to someone who wasn't normal?

There were only ten people in front of me when the dairy owner stepped outside to lower the metal grating over the window with a thud. "Hey!" people shouted. "What are you doing? What's going on?" The first ones in line, those who were about to enter, explained: Don Ramón had run out of butter.

This is so awful. Stop jerking us around. Imagine standing out here in the cold and wasting our time for nothing. Some complained loudly, while some threw themselves against the dairy owner as though it were his fault after all.

Little by little they began to disperse. Some remained behind talking and complaining, among them the pedicurist's son, who seemed to have forgotten that he had already been in line and had in fact managed to get some butter. He complained as bitterly as those at the end of the line. When everyone else finally left, he stood alone in front of the metal grating and began to shout: "You shiddy bastuhd! Gimme budder!"

As I walked away, I could still hear him shouting, "Oben ub, you shiddy bastuhd! Gimme budder!"

YOU CAN LIVE WITHOUT BUTTER. YOU CAN LIVE WITHOUT sugar, even without a stove. It's just a matter of throwing a few more rags on your shoulders, wearing warm slippers and going to bed early with a hot-water bottle and a good book. There's never a shortage of books.

The cold in the street is less biting than in the house. On the streetcars people travel so crowded together there's no room for the cold. The subway is a pleasure. I get off at Piedras and get in the line for Suipacha. I always stand in front of the same shop window, always look at the same coral sweater.

I enter San Miguel Church. The pleasure I get from churches grows more intense all the time. This is an opulent church: I enjoy spending a little while here in the morning before going to school. I sit in the pew, look at the statues, breathe in the incense, and spy on the movements of those women who begin their day in church.

I've already pulled the piece of mosquito netting out of my pocket (so no bitch of a little old lady can come over and tell me how disrespectful I'm being to God), and put it on my head. None of these women has a head covering much better than mine; I don't have to feel ashamed. Some of them come in from the street with a kerchief already tied under their chin. That doesn't seem sufficiently religious to me. You should cover your head right in the church doorway, to differentiate being inside the church from being outside. What they're doing is like lighting an electric bulb for the Virgin instead of a candle.

By now I'm such a good friend of God's that I know he won't get angry with me if I'm distracted by what the women are wearing on their heads. There's a skinny one, fairly young, with a pretty lace mantilla. She's praying very energetically, crossing herself every few minutes. Seems to be in a hurry.

Some women are wearing very simple veils, but none of them reveals its mosquito-netting origin as obviously as mine does. Luckily, the church is a dark place, and as long as you have something on your head, no one notices.

I keep scanning heads to see if I can find anyone even poorer than I am.

I found her. She's bent over the last pew, and she's placed a bundle beside her, made of paper and rags. On her head there's no mantilla, no kerchief tied beneath her chin, not even a piece of mosquito netting. She has a piece of newspaper on her head. She's not kneeling, not praying, not crossing herself. She's simply sitting, with her bundle of rags by her side and the open newspaper on her head.

Simply sitting, looking at God, goddammit.

YOU'RE PROBABLY ASKING YOURSELF: WHAT'S THIS JEW doing in my church? Why doesn't she go to her own and leave us alone?

I'll tell you why: because I don't know it. Once I was in a synagogue, at a fancy wedding. It was one of the most beautiful synagogues in Buenos Aires. But it was very stripped down; there was nothing to see.

I know tons about the Catholic religion: I know prayers, I know gestures, I know Jesus. I go to church in secret, and that makes the pleasure all the greater. I couldn't go into a synagogue in secret: some relative would see me and shout out hello. And my religion, whatever it may be, has to be a secret, because deep down I'm an atheist. My head is devoid of illusions: when I die, I die, and there's nothing on the other side. Only a dreamless sleep. That's what I learned from my grandfather, the one who wanted to be cremated. "We're nothing," he said. And his body, which he nurtured only with vegetables, which he draped over a chair to read *La Vanguardia*, turned out to be such a negligible thing that it all fit into a little box, a little box which occasionally caused upsets.

"I've come to remind you to go to the cemetery to visit Papa," Mele said. It's been ten years, and if we don't pay the bill they're going to send him to the Paupers' Graveyard."

No one could go. No one had time. Everyone thought the others should go, and all of them were such prima donnas, and they started to argue about who went the last time, and by the end of the argument it was clear that they were fighting over something that had nothing to do with Grandpa or with the cemetery. I was afraid they'd forget, that they wouldn't rescue him, and what was left of Grandpa would be lost forever.

I think he did get lost. I don't know where the little box is, if it's anywhere, and I don't have the courage to ask.

You're probably thinking: "Why are you giving me all this bullshit about cemeteries and things like that? Isn't it bad enough you use my church and reject your own? Why should I give a shit about your grandfather's ashes? And for that matter, what difference does it make what happens to the dead?"

AND NOW, LIKE EVERY OTHER DAY AT THE SAME TIME, the sports bulletin comes on the air:

Garibaldi, Garibaldi, Garibaldi!
Boom!
Garibaldi!
Boom!
Garibaldi!
Boom!
Garibaldi, Garibaldi, Garibaldi!
Boom!
Garibaldi!
Boom! Boom! Boom!

"But why?"

"'Cause I don't feel like it."

"But why?"

"I don't know why."

"But I only want you to tell me why."

"'Cause I don't wanna, cause I don't wanna, cause I don't feel like it."

"I don't care if you don't eat, but I want you to tell me why."

"'Cause I don't wanna, 'cause I don't wanna, 'cause I don't feel like it, Mama."

And out I go into the street, with that expression of mine: a sideways glance, unblinking. Could it be in this building, could it be in this office? Could this be the office of the Manager?

"It's here, it's here," I'll tell her confidently. "Here it is."

Take the elevator up. Elevator. Elevator operator. Which floor? Tenth. Are you going up, too? Me too. Go on, go on. Go on, please, looking sideways with that face of yours. So you're going up, too? I'm going up, I'm going all the way up. Is it this door? No, miss, it's the one next to it. Is the Manager in? There's no one here. What do you mean, no one here? Today the lady is in. What lady? Well, the Manager has one of those ladies who clean offices. I'm not looking for any lady. I'm looking for the Manager. But the lady isn't in, anyway. She isn't? She was here before! She must've left. But even if she didn't leave, what am I supposed to say to her?

"Could you please tell me?"

"Weren't you looking for the Manager's office?"

"But I wasn't looking for an office, I was looking for the Manager. Couldn't you please tell me?"

"I couldn't say."

"Where's the Paupers' Graveyard?"

"That information you'll have to ask the Manager."

In that case, excuse me, excuse me, and hand me that broom. Thanks again, thank you, don't worry about it, thank you, thanks a lot. Roses, flutes, nausea, a solitary clock with its axis broken for the hundredth time, good-bye, and on my way.

"NO CHILDREN," SAID MY GRANDMOTHER. "WHY BRING more unhappiness into the world?" Mele, who had finally gotten married, didn't plan on having a baby, like other married women.

That raised two questions: First, could Mele have had children at her age, even if she wanted to? Second, what did Grandma mean by "bringing more unhappiness into the world?" Did she think Mele's children would be unhappy? Unhappy because they had old parents? Or rather did Grandma think that any child who came into the world, Mele's or otherwise, would be unhappy? Unhappy because another catastrophe was about to happen? Another war? The end of the world? Unhappy because we Jews are all unhappy? Or all the members of our family?

I couldn't ask any of these questions aloud, because I wasn't supposed to be eavesdropping on the conversation. I was supposed to be in my room, learning the theorem that says A is equal to A, which can be proven through absurdity.

Grandma and the sister of Leon the Watchmaker, the one who had a crazy daughter in the asylum, had brought their chairs out to the patio and were sitting there talking and shaking their heads in the conventional manner that denotes sadness.

The truth is that Mele looked very happy whenever she left the house with her husband, Uncle Tomás (Tevye to his friends), a timid man with gray hair and a gray mustache, and a certain hesitancy in saying what he did for a living. I found out (through conversations I wasn't supposed to overhear) that he worked at a window at the racetrack. I don't know exactly what was wrong with having that job, but he probably knew, since he avoided discussing it. Or maybe he felt eclipsed by our family, which, even though it was going through some hard times, was an illustrious one, where everyone had always been musicians and watchmakers since the time of King David himself ("Musician" means liturgical cantor in the synagogue, and "watchmaker" means watch repairman. There never was a butcher or a tailor in the family to tarnish the luster of our lineage).

During their courtship, Mele received Tomás's visits every Sunday in the dining room. He always brought cream meringues for tea. For a few months after the wedding, they lived with us. They occupied the bedroom that faced the street, about a hundred feet from the bathroom. Whenever Mele and Mama had a fight, Mama would lock the door to the dining room, which was the only covered passageway to the bathroom. If it was cold or raining, this was a serious inconvenience. When it rained, Tomás would run across the patio, sheltering himself under a big umbrella. He had a strange way of running, Tomás did. He ran with tiny steps, all hunched over, making so little progress that I couldn't understand why he bothered to run: he would have gotten there just as fast by walking. Mele explained it to me confidentially one afternoon, when she told me Tomás's story.

When Tomás was a boy over in Poland, his father taught him to work in the fields. If Tomás did something wrong, or if he got tired, his father would beat him with the same whip he used to prod the horses. It was useless for Tomás to try to escape: a man can run faster than a boy, and there was Tomás, running with his baby steps, his back hunched over, beneath his father's whip. After I heard this story, whenever I saw Tomás running across the patio, I turned away.

As soon as they were able, Mele and Tomás moved out and rented a small apartment. They crammed it so full of furniture you couldn't even walk, so Tomás couldn't run in there, even if he had wanted to.

This autumnal marriage was, without a doubt, the happiest one our family ever had.

"YOU'RE FILTHY RICH. TAKE CARE OF YOUR MOTHER."

That was the end of the conversation. Mama slammed down the receiver. Grandma moved out a week later, escorted by Clark Gable, who carried her valise. After that, Mama and Otilia were estranged for a long time. Otilia made several fruitless attempts to send Grandma back to us.

I visited Grandma from time to time. I found her very worn out, vacant, or displaying symptoms of that strange disease which had affected her from time immemorial, and which no doctor could ever pinpoint. Everyone thought she seemed healthy, remarkably healthy for her age, and at the very most, they prescribed vitamins for her. "Doctors don't know anything," she insisted, following her own prescriptions. A medical student from the neighborhood came over whenever she called him to give her injections or to take her blood pressure. Sitting at her side, he would proceed to extract the blood pressure device parsimoniously from his bag. He'd place it on her arm, which she, adept at this sort of thing, allowed to hang limply off the side of the bed, and meanwhile they would chat about any old thing: if it was hot or cold, or about some plant on the patio. Then the young man would tell Grandma the numerical reading on the blood pressure device, and that would determine the climate that reigned in the household for the next few days. Even when her pressure was normal, Grandma was a time bomb. Any unpleasantness, a fight, and her pressure could shoot up and kill her. "You're going to kill me," she intoned sweetly whenever anyone annoyed her.

ONCE A YEAR, ON A CERTAIN DATE, THERE IS A BIG PARTY at the Israelite Home for the Aged. They deck out the old people in their best finery, and they invite the whole Jewish community to spend Sunday at the institution. This provides an opportunity for a festive social occasion. They set up picnic tables, food and drink booths, coat rooms and donation ladders. Whoever gives the largest donation gets to climb to the highest rung. Ever since their financial situation changed, Otilia and Clark Gable never missed a chance to donate, unlike our family, which remained chronically wretched. But none of this matters to us, because we're intellectuals, whereas they—at best, and even this is pushing it—are bourgeois pigs.

After she assumed responsibility for her mother, Otilia began to see the nursing home in a different light. She began to pay less attention to the jewels worn by the visitors, or to the pile of contributions made by the Ladies' Auxiliary of the Israelite Home for the Aged, and more attention to the faces of the residents and how they lived. "Never," she proclaimed impetuously after this inspection. However, every time Grandma became unmanageable, she resumed arguing with her sisters so that they, too, would take some responsibility for their mother. The only thing she managed to accomplish in all the years Grandma lived in her house was a three month respite which Grandma spent with Amanda in General Pico. At the end of this period, Amanda sent her back on the pretext that she herself was ill.

Grandma didn't die of high blood pressure. While in her eighties (although she never admitted to more than seventy-eight) she underwent an operation. By that time

I was already far away from her, from everything. I found out by telephone that she was sick and was going to have an operation. I also found out by telephone that she had died.

The coffin, closed according to Hebrew custom, and covered with a black cloth with the Star of David on it, was laid out in a rented funeral parlor. I don't believe this was done according to her expressed desires. It would have been impossible for her to make arrangements for her demise, since she never believed in it, unlike Grandpa, who believed in Ideas and in Absolute Death, and wanted to burn up into Nothingness to prove it. The idea of burying Grandma according to Jewish custom must have been Otilia's, as she couldn't stand jeopardizing her relationship with the Jewish community.

It was raining when they removed the casket from the funeral parlor to transport it to La Tablada cemetery. It rained while we waited for them to wash the corpse and carry it into the temple.

The ceremony was brief. Standing around the casket, we listened to the rabbi's lamentations in Hebrew. Although we didn't understand them, this ceremony was the most beautiful event Grandma ever starred in. Then, as the rain continued, they buried her, in a place very far from the entrance. The best spots, those that face the main street, were spoken for long ago. They are reserved for the famous dead, who, even though they're still alive, know how to stake their claim.